Enjoy

Debra Dixon

Sweet Tea And Jesus Shoes

Donna Ball
Sandra Chastain
Debra Dixon *Laura Austin's daughter*
Virginia Ellis
Nancy Knight
Deborah Smith

copyright 2000 by BelleBooks
ISBN: 0-9673035-0-8

BelleBooks

P.O. Box 67
Smyrna, GA 30081

Bellebooks@BelleBooks.com

Cover Design by Virginia Ellis
Cover photograph (c) Gin Stamm

Sweet Tea and Jesus Shoes

Never let the truth stand in the way of a good story.
—unknown

Table of Contents

PRECIOUS MEMORIES

THE JESUS SHOES

by Sandra Chastain

No one can make you feel inferior without your consent.
—Eleanor Roosevelt

T he rituals of the summer of 1945 were observed even in the midst of a war about which I knew little. I was too young to understand the supper table talk about war, yet old enough to cherish the rhythm of summer: wading in the creek that ran through the big ditch, picking blackberries, churning ice cream, and Vacation Bible School.

For me, at age eight, Vacation Bible School started with a pair of new white patent-leather sandals with little silver buckles. Shoes were rationed and I, in my sublime ignorance, had no idea of the sacrifices my grandparents made to provide those sandals. No matter that my body was adorned with sun dresses made from chicken feed sacks, my patent-leather clad feet were on the Glory Road.

On the second Monday morning in June, I headed for the Wadley Methodist Church. Walking alone was safe then, even for a child. Tires and gasoline were rationed so there was little traffic, and only

9

one stop light in town. To save energy, that traffic light had been turned off, which didn't matter because everyone knew to stop at the intersection, and we did. Everyone, that is, except for the convoys of army trucks that came through, carrying soldiers who waved at all of us. My grandmother always walked toward the highway and waved back. "Somebody, somewhere is doing that for one of our boys," she'd say.

But that morning, there were no convoys and no traffic and I was glad because I didn't want to take to the side of the road where beggar lice might stick to my dress, or worse yet, dust might mar my shiny new shoes. The sun had already turned the blue-black asphalt into soft, bubbly patches and heat rose in waves that seemed to breathe. I concentrated on keeping my eyes on my shoes. I was used to the heat and an expert at curving my lower lip to blow the ever present swarm of gnats out of my line of vision. And nothing was going to stop my annual attendance at Vacation Bible School. Neither gnats nor tar bubbles were going to prevent me from reaching the church in my pristine white sandals.

My best friend, Rachel, was waiting for me on the graveled parking area by the side of the church. After she spent some time admiring my shoes, we joined hands and skipped up the steps.

Miss Bessie Newton met us at the door, wearing her usual starched print dress sprinkled around the collar with pink face powder that smelled of roses. Miss Bessie had what my grandmother called the biggest dinner table in town. Years later that I found out she was referring to the twin peaks of her anatomy and not the size of her furniture.

If the top of Miss Bessie was oversized, the bottom of her didn't match. Looking at her shoes that morning, I whispered to Rachel that her feet were no bigger than my size four. Behind her hand, Rachel confided solemnly that Miss Bessie hadn't seen her feet since she was thirteen. I giggled on the way in and got frowned at by Miss Bessie.

Once inside, Rachel and I were herded to the proper room where eight other children had already gathered. I knew six of them. We'd gone to school and church together all our lives.

The other two were strangers, both boys.

They'd just moved to Wadley, and they came to the church barefoot. Now there was nothing un-usual about children going barefoot in the south; we all did. But never to church. That was considered dis-respectful.

Still, Miss Bessie welcomed them and assigned them to my class, which was called the Soldiers of the Cross. We learned the boys were Hansel and Willie Mosely who had come to stay with their great Aunt Louella.

Rachel and I stared at the boys in amazement. Not only did they *not* wear shoes to church, a sure sign of their lack of breeding, but their feet were dirty. The younger one, in fact, hadn't even been as careful with his feet as I had been with my shoes. He had tar between his toes and dirt caked on his bare heels. Both boys' hair stuck up every which-a-way and it looked like Miss Louella, who was poor and couldn't see very well, had given them a haircut with her rusty old push mower.

We'd been taught to be kind to the poor, but to my certain knowledge, nobody had ever sanctioned

11

dirty feet and choppy hair.

Feeling the stern training of my grandmother and a nudge from Miss Bessie, I stepped forward and held out my hand. "I'm Sandra Anglin and I'm pleased to meet you."

They didn't shake my hand. But I'd done my Christian duty.

I had to remember that Christian duty again when we started to the auditorium for the opening session and one of the boys stepped square on my new white sandal with his dirty foot and left a long smear of black tar streaking one toe. I bent down and rubbed the underside of my sundress hem across the tar, only making it worse. Like a martyr, I stood looking at my pitiful, scarred shoe, my anger growing with every minute.

I determined that he should be punished for his transgressions. An eye for an eye. But since he didn't have any shoes to scar in return, I had to think of something else.

After we'd been told the schedule and reminded that on Friday we would present a program in the church for the entire congregation, which would be followed by a picnic, we were sent to our first class.

The Soldiers of the Cross met in the largest adult classroom because we were tall enough to sit in the adult chairs at the tables used by the regular Sunday School Classes. As always, we would study Scriptures and hear Bible stories for the first hour. The second hour was reserved for crafts, and I looked forward this summer session to my first year of spatter painting. I'd even brought an old toothbrush of my own to use.

My older sister's spatter painting was a work

of art still tacked to the wall over my grandmother's iron bed. She'd used white shoe polish, she said, carefully dipping her toothbrush into the polish and rubbing it over a piece of screen wire so that the spray of white spattered to outline the large leaf from an oak tree placed on a piece of red construction paper below. I was too young to even understand the complexities of her work, she'd assured me. For two years I'd considered how to outdo her and had finally chosen black polish sprinkled over two, five-pointed leaves from a sweet gum tree on pink paper. It would be a glorious creation, surpassing her puny effort totally.

But to add insult to the injury already done to my new shoes, I learned that our curriculum had been changed. Toothbrushes and shoe polish were hard to come by so a new project had been devised for the Soldiers of the Cross. This year, we'd make shoes like Jesus wore.

I objected, to no avail, and decided that this was another test of my Christian training. I'd waited two years for my turn to spatter paint and it was not to be.

The change in curriculum suited the two new boys just fine. They thought Jesus Shoes were perfect, another of their quickly mounting transgressions. It was clear to me they knew nothing of tradition. Due primarily to my urging, the other children sided with me in somehow blaming them for the fact that we would not be doing spatter prints for the first time since anyone could remember.

Hansel and Willie clung together for the next five days, and the rest of us tormented them at every opportunity. They wore the same shirts and shorts every day and their feet only got dirtier. Miss Bessie privately scolded us for our attitude toward two home-less children who were being cared for by an elderly woman who was poor and almost blind, but we were unheeding. As Soldiers of the Cross, we felt called to see that these boys be returned to wherever they'd come from. They clearly didn't belong here.

When simple shunning didn't work, we accidentally knocked over their glue, gave them the dullest scissors, refused to share our supplies. Still, in spite of the sabotage attempts launched by my little band of followers, the Jesus Shoes project went forward.

Each of us drew an outline of our feet on brown paper to be used as a pattern. Then from an assortment of fertilizer sacks and quilt scraps, we used our brown paper bag patterns to cut more soles. The cutting, with blunt-edged scissors, was a laborious process that took two days.

Once we had the soles, we met our next challenge: punching the holes through which our ties would be strung. Ice picks and large nails worked best—until one earnest Soldier pounded the nail through the layers of soles and into the floor.

The Mosley boys managed fine, but Miss Bessie finally had to find a male assistant to give us a hand until all the holes were punched. Then came the glue, made from flour, water and a bit of rosin collected from local pine trees. Matching our holes, we cemented the layers together to make thick soles.

By Thursday, the shoes were complete and ready for the threading of the rope that would criss-cross the bottom of the shoes and come across the wearer's foot, then up the leg. After trying them on, it was my opinion that the reason all the apostles had such sad expressions in their pictures was because their feet hurt.

Friday brought assembly and a presentation by the individual classes. Our class was to sing the song from which we acquired our name, *Onward Christian Soldiers*. It was when we were lining up to go into the church that Miss Louella shuffled up the sidewalk to where Miss Bessie was standing. We all turned to stare.

In a timid voice the boys' aunt thanked Miss Bessie for looking after her nephews. Their mother had been killed in the same house fire that had destroyed most of their clothing and toys. Their father was missing in action in the South Pacific. It was hard, she said, but taking them in was the Christian thing for her to do.

She said they'd come home every day talking about how kind the children had been and how much fun they'd had in Vacation Bible School. She particularly wanted to thank *me*.

Every Christian Soldier in line heard her and turned their eyes on me. My heart hurt and my face burned. I couldn't look at them. I ducked my head and saw the boys' feet and my own, which were still adorned in the nearly new white patent leather sandals. I knew I had to make amends, but I couldn't think how until Miss Bessie began lining us up to march into the sanctuary.

I pulled the boys forward and gave Willie the cross I'd been assigned to carry. Then I knelt, removed my white sandals and left them on the steps when I took my place behind the boys, barefoot. One by one, the others took off their shoes, including Miss Bessie, who'd never gone barefoot in her life before. We marched on naked feet to the altar where we sat down and put on our Jesus shoes, then stood and sang our song, "Onward Christian Soldiers, marching as to war, with the cross of Jesus going on before."

●●●

Hansel and Willie lived with their aunt until she died and remained inseparable thereafter. They entered the army together and served in the Korean war, where both were killed in action. I never forgot them. My white patent leather sandals with the silver buckles and scarred toe are long gone, but I still have those Jesus shoes.

NO MORE MICKEY MOUSE

by Virginia Ellis

It all started with a mouse.
—Walt Disney

My grandmother moved in with us when I was about five years old. We lived in an old farmhouse aways out in the country with indoor plumbing and well water; with electricity but only one serious gas heater and a bunch of quilts to keep us warm.

I didn't know it then, but I guess we were poor.

My grandmother knew it, however. Even as young as I was, I got the impression that our grandmother thought she'd been destined for better things than living with her son's working wife and her three wild-Indian children. To this day I don't have the nerve to call her Grandma, that would be disrespectful. Her friends called her Miss Alma. I usually just said, "Yes, ma'am."

A fire and brimstone Baptist, Miss Alma never missed a Sunday service and never got dressed-up without wearing what looked like a corset, hose, and pumps with heels. Not to mention a hat.

Dire circumstances must have brought her, along with her black and white Zenith TV and her caged canary, to our house—a place where we kids rarely wore shoes and chickens roamed the yard. I knew that my Grandpa had died years before and Grandmother had been living in her own house in the city. No one ever told me why she sold that house and moved to the sticks. But whatever the reason, I don't believe it was a happy one.

From the first day she arrived a new order took over our household. She would fix us breakfast, and *we would eat it.* Burnt toast along with burnt bacon. Burnt toast with guava jelly and burnt bacon. You get the picture. My grandmother couldn't cook. We couldn't beg for store bought cereal or unburnt toast. Miss Alma didn't have a lot of patience for picky children. The axiom from the Bible, "Spare the rod, spoil the child," rang true in her heart. It rang true on my nether-end more than a few times, too.

Another sort of order came in terms of television time. We were allowed to watch the *Mickey Mouse Club* in the afternoons as long as we didn't bother Grandmother during her soap operas. Her *stories* she called them. If memory serves me, it was *The Guiding Light* she especially loved.

Not bothering my grandmother was easy—much easier than the consequences of being a pest. Given our preference, my sister and I would far rather be outside building forts, trying to catch birds with a box and a stick, or climbing up into the old dilapidated barn to see the baby owls. We were also known for sneaking our dog upstairs into the attic so he could crash around like a bumper car as he chased rats. We didn't do that when our grandmother was watching television, however, or we'd have never seen Mickey again.

One of the things my grandmother *could* do was crochet. To this day I have not seen any crochet work I would say was any better than hers. Not long after settling in with us, Miss Alma organized some of the women in the church into a circle. They would quilt or crochet items to be auctioned off for charity. Every few weeks the circle would visit our house, and sometimes I would be still and quiet in order to be allowed to sit on the floor by Grandmother's chair and watch them work.

On one particular Wednesday afternoon the six ladies arrived as usual carrying their sewing bags and wearing aprons or pin cushions on their wrists. Two of them brought along Campbell Soup cans which they set on the floor next to their chairs so they could raise them and spit. I once asked one of them why she did that, and instead of explaining the physical process of dipping snuff, she told me, "Because it's impolite to spit in the sink."

Now, I believe I have already mentioned the rats in the attic. For the squeamish I suppose I could call them mice. But those of you who have ever lived in the country with farm animals in the vicinity know the kind of rats I'm talking about. Mickey Mouse might have them in size, but not by much.

Well, on that Wednesday, the circle sat down and commenced to crochet. They were making a spectacular double bed cover out of crocheted squares that looked like pink spider webs. Each square had a three dimensional rose complete with petals and leaves in it. It was the most beautiful thing I had ever seen.

Miss Alma was sitting a few feet from the wall

near a lamp table, and I sat on the floor next to her. She'd let me use one of her crochet needles to knot up thread. I remember occasional conversation among them but the subject didn't register. I was busy pretending to make some of the rose squares, confident mine would look as perfect as the others. Then Grandmother instructed me to get up and turn on the TV for her soap opera. I stopped my crocheting and did as I was told.

The show was almost over when the rat appeared.

My attention had drifted away from the Ivory Snow commercial on the TV, and I happened to look past my grandmother where I saw almost face to face, since he was on the end table, a rat the size of a Chihuahua. This estimation of size could have been due to the fact I'd never been nearly eyeball to eyeball to one. Before I could squeak out a warning, the rat leaped right onto my grandmother's lap.

You know how sometimes in stressful situations the actions around you shift into slow motion? That's what happened as I watched the rat land. I expected Miss Alma to shout and shake the thing off her. But my grandmother, without dropping a stitch or making a sound, calmly backhanded the rat so hard it flew over my head and hit the wall behind me with a thud.

I waited for everyone else to scream and run like sixty, like I wanted to do—and as I was sure the rat had done. But not a word was spoken. I saw one lady reach down and lift her soup can off the floor and set it on a table. The other woman soon followed suit with her can. Then *The Guiding Light* came back on and the incident passed like I'd imagined the whole thing.

Now, you've got to admire that kind of utter calm in the face of a rat attack. But what happened later further proved the point that interrupting Grandmother could be hazardous to your health if you're a rat.

After the ladies had gone home and Grandmother was in the kitchen burning dinner, I heard my sister scream, "Rat!" from the front room. Before I could laugh at her predicament, the rat came racing around the corner into the bedroom I was in. I screamed and climbed up on the top bed of our bunk beds.

It looked like this rat had lost his map of how to get back to his friends in the attic. Unfortunately, that meant we were stuck with him.

I heard my grandmother asking, "Where is he?" My sister blubbered out something. Then grandmother looked in my door. She had a broom in her hand.

"He went that way." I pointed, perfectly willing to help as long as I didn't have to get down off my perch.

A few minutes later, after some shuffling and banging of furniture, Grandmother called my sister into the kitchen. For once I was glad to be the younger child. But, after a few minutes of silence, my curiosity got the better of me. I went into the kitchen in time to hear my grandmother instructing my sister. "Now you hold that cabinet closed. I'll be right back."

As she went out the back door to the porch, my sister screwed up her face and said, "The rat's in there." She had one finger firmly placed on the cabinet and was stretched as far as possible away from it in case she needed to run.

Before I could get past the fact that we'd actually caught him and wonder what the heck we were going to do with him, my grandmother returned.

She had a hatchet in her hand.

"Now I want you to open that door then get out of the way," she said to my sister.

My sister looked at me and I swear her eyes were as big as an owl's. An owl who'd stuck its toe in an electric socket.

"You get back out of the way, too," Grandmother said to me.

The main thing I knew I had to do was get out of my sister's way. 'Cause when she opened that cabinet I had no doubt she wouldn't stop running till she'd cleared the front door, and I didn't want to be flattened in the process.

I knew better than to argue with my grandmother, and certainly choosing a time when she had a hatchet in her hand would be dumber than dirt.

I backed up.

My sister slapped the cabinet open and hightailed it. But she surprised me; she stopped at the kitchen door. We both needed to see what would happen, I guess—if for no other reason than to be able to tell our mother when she got home from work.

It didn't take long. The rat jumped out, escape rather than attack on his mind, and Grandmother cleaved him with the first try.

In later days, I probably would have said, "Cool." Then, I stayed as quiet as a...rabbit.

Grandmother gave one indignant sniff as she picked up the barely connected rat by the tail and took it and the bloody hatchet out the back door.

"This creature won't bother us again," she said.

I would like to think that Grandmother killed the rat to protect us. But within a short time I realized the rat had paid the ultimate price for interrupting Grandmother and her soap opera.

No more Mickey Mouse.

NOLA'S ASHES

by Deborah Smith

The heart's dead are never buried.
—Samuel Hoffenstein

L ike most southern women, I was often the referee for two opposing teams—Mama's side of the family, and Daddy's side of the family. We abbreviated the terms and rolled the key words together as a shorthand to make the distinctions easier. Mamaside. Daddyside. For example, my mama's mother used to say: The young'uns on your Mamaside never think to poke things up their noses for fun. But the young'uns on your Daddyside will stick a dadblame crawfish up their snout if you let 'em.

Great Aunt Nola was from Daddyside, the eldest of my grandmother and her five sisters. She, Grandmother, and the rest were all ill-tempered and domineering, but as their ringleader, Nola had no equal in the bad-mood sweepstakes. She was the worst-case example of my hard-headed Daddyside kin. Nola, Grandmother, and their sisters had, on average, a good seventy-five years of things to fight about. Who got to wear the nicest dress to the revival meeting one summer. What really happened the night in

1942 when Cousin Seeton got hit by the train? Had Papa's favorite mule been named Glory or Beau? When Uncle John came home from Korea, who was he happiest to see? They went round after round by phone and mail over those and other issues, both lesser and greater. Since my grandmother lived with us, we regularly heard the loud, unpleasant phone battles from her bedroom.

"Thank God," my mama said. "All but two of the old biddies live out of state. I can't imagine acting that way with my sisters."

You see, on Mamaside there was civility, kindness, and true camaraderie among siblings. Mama and her four sisters never even raised their voices to each other. So the rantings among the women of Daddyside not only distressed Mama, they disgusted her. Not that Daddy approved of his mother's relationship with her sisters, either. He dreaded the rare occasions when one or more of his aunts came to visit Grandma, because invariably the visit would break down into a yelling match within hours, and then Daddy would have to get the car and load up the visiting sisters and drive them back to their homes or to the Greyhound Bus station. I can't recall a single visit in which a sister actually ended up spending the night as planned.

This kind of nonsense wore thin over the years. Daddy died young of a heart attack, leaving Mama to deal with Grandma and her sisters alone. I decided to help her as much as I could, so after I married and moved nearby, I ran interference as often as possible: intercepting phone calls, chauffeuring angry visiting sisters back to the bus station or the airport, and writing obligatory birthday and Christmas cards Mama refused to send. She blamed Daddy's early heart attack on stress induced, in part, by Grandma and her sisters.

Mama watched with quiet glee as three of the Daddyside sisters died off. Then Grandma passed away, leaving only Nola, who was eighty-seven and lived in a small apartment an hour's drive away, in Atlanta. Nola had divorced her two husbands decades earlier, never had any children, and for the past twenty years had refused to travel farther than a mile from her apartment building. Which meant that whenever I had been pressed into service driving Grandma to visit Nola for lunch, we could not eat at Grandma's favorite place, the Picadilly Cafeteria, because it was on the other side of the intersection that marked the boundaries of Nola's territory. And every time, Grandma and Nola would argue about Nola's eccentricity.

When Grandma died, I thought, I'll never have to hear about the "twenty damned feet of concrete between here and the Picadilly," again. I sent Great Aunt Nola money for her birthday and Christmas, and every month or so during the rest of the year, with cards saying, "Have a nice lunch on me, and call me if you need anything," so Nola wouldn't bother Mama. Nola started calling me at least once a week to fill me in on all the issues she and Grandma and the sisters had argued over. I felt sorry for her. She couldn't stop arguing, even if there was no one left to argue with. She was a prizefighter swinging gamely in the middle of an empty ring. I wasn't good for anything but listening—no yelling, no slinging the phone—but I would do for practice.

"You stay out of Nola's business, because I've already done my duty and you've done yours to all the old ladies from your Daddyside," Mama said regularly, never suspecting that I was paying Nola hush money and diverting her punches.

One day, Nola died. Just died in her sleep, nothing extravagant about it, and I was grateful that my duty had finally ended. But then I realized that because she had no blood relatives other than me—a great niece—I had to take charge of the funeral. Nola had attached a note to her will, saying she didn't want any ceremonies, she just wanted her body cremated, and she wanted me to pay for it, but giving no other instructions. When Mama saw the will, she said in disgust, "Well, I'll be damned."

Nola left all her apartment furnishings, her small savings account, and her '67 Buick to an old man who lived in the apartment next door to hers. I didn't know if she considered him her boyfriend or not, and I didn't ask.

"Lord, lord," he said when I told him about the legacy. "That car hasn't been out of the garage in ten years. She sure didn't like to travel."

"Would you like for me to send you her ashes?" I asked hopefully. "I mean, to keep in an urn, in honor of her memory, or maybe to sprinkle in the shrubs outside your building, or something like that?"

"Oh, no," he answered quickly. "The Buick's enough for me."

When I told Mama, she snorted, "I'll be damned," again.

She and I had to go down to the funeral home and set up the paperwork for the cremation, and we had to identify Nola's body as a matter of formality. Mama preceded me into the viewing room with an unlit cigarette clamped in her lips. She squinted at

Nola's corpse, which had been wrapped artfully in white sheets. "Yeah, that's her," she growled to the mortuary director. As we walked out, Mama said to me, "She looks like all the old ladies on your Daddyside. Good and dead."

Unlike Mama, I regarded my Daddyside duties with stoic neutrality. I was just glad Nola wouldn't be calling me anymore. I merely wanted to disperse her ashes and pay off her phone bill. I called some of her elderly distant cousins, and I called her few remaining old friends. Surely one of them would feel honored and compelled to accept Nola's dusty remains. No sale.

After a week or so the impatient funeral director called. "I'm sorry," he said, "but I can't store your great aunt's remains any longer. I'll ship them to you by regular mail."

"I have an oversized m-mailbox," I stuttered in surprise, "but I'm not sure—"

"We do this kind of thing all the time. The remains will be safely packaged in a small, plain-brown box. They'll fit."

I began to watch the mailbox nervously. Four days later, the package still hadn't arrived. My husband and I lived on a secluded country road. With a certain amount of grim humor he pointed to an article in our small town weekly newspaper. *Post Office Reports Mail Thefts In Some Areas*. Oh, no. Maybe someone had stolen Great Aunt Nola.

"They probably mistook the plain-brown package for dirty movies," Mama said.

Two weeks later, the post office located the package in the mailbox of a recently vacated house trailer on the other side of the county. Our new 911 system had instituted new street addresses only a month before, and my address and the other were only one digit different.

At any rate, when I retrieved the package from the post office I suddenly realized how strange it felt to hold a small cardboard box, knowing that, in a very real sense, Great Aunt Nola was inside. I could remember all her pettiness, and all the bickering of the Daddyside sisters in general, all their disregard for simple civility and larger purposes, and how much misery they had caused Daddy. Bad feelings seemed to gather around that box like a smell.

I couldn't bear to store it in my house until I decided what to do with the ashes. My husband refused to take it to his office, saying his secretary dutifully opened and unpacked every package she found near his desk and wouldn't like the surprise if she accidentally dumped Great Aunt Nola on the carpet. So I set the box in the back of my Explorer and drove over to Mama's.

"The old lady's ashes don't worry me," Mama grunted. She pointed to a wheelbarrow in her garage. "Just set 'em over there."

"I can't just put Great Aunt Nola in the wheelbarrow!"

Mama rummaged in a closet then handed me a glossy, green, Rich's Department Store bag. "Put it in that first," she ordered. "Then anybody who walks by will think I've been shopping."

I gave up. The box went into the bag, and I set the bag in the wheelbarrow. This just wasn't right; it wasn't decent; it wasn't respectful, I told myself. Yet I was glad to get the box out of my vehicle and safely stored in the garage.

Where, the next day, it was stolen by Joey Abercrombie, the boy who mowed Mama's lawn.

She noticed the bag missing not long after Joey cut the grass. He was only eight years old, and not mean, just not particularly bright. Mama called his mother, who shrieked, "He did what?" and then in the background Mama could hear the sound of her flailing Joey, and Joey yelping.

When Joey's mother returned the box—un-opened, thank goodness—she told Mama that Joey thought the box looked like it might have dirty movies in it.

I couldn't take this grisly and bizarre responsibility any longer. I decided to transport Great Aunt Nola to the small town at the south end of the state where she and all of Daddyside had been born. It was a five-hour drive, but once there I'd locate the old town cemetery and sprinkle Great Aunt Nola's ashes on the graves of her parents, my great-grandparents. Mama insisted on going with me. We went on a summer Saturday, with thunderstorms crossing our path between alternate periods of hot, damp sunshine. It was late afternoon by the time we reached Daddyside's hometown and found the cemetery. It had the quiet, pastoral look of all old rural cemeteries, where the grass is faded and a little bare in places, and the old headstones are surrounded by lovingly tended shrubs or ornamental fences.

I carried the box to a pair of worn gray tombstones with my great-grandparents' names on them. Mama kept her distance. This was not her blood family; this was not her sentiment. When we'd left that morning she'd offered one last suggestion: "If you won't tell anybody," she said, "I'll flush Great Aunt

Nola down my commode, and that'll be the end of it."

But I insisted on this small propriety, and so she had come along for my sake—but chain-smoking, grimacing, and turning the car radio to loud and profane stations she never listened to ordinarily. When I wrestled with the box's tape, she tossed me the pen knife she kept in her purse. "Just cut it," she said. "The wind's coming up."

Something unfurled inside me. With our duty to Daddyside almost done, I stopped cold with the half-opened box in one hand, faced my mother, and said something I had held quietly in my heart for many years.

"You've let them turn you into a bitter woman," I told her, and began to cry. "You've turned into a Daddyside person, and I want you back the way you ought to be."

She began to cry, too, and came to me, and we hugged, trying not to squeeze the box full of Aunt Nola between us. "It's over," she promised.

I nodded. There was nothing else to say about wounds so deep.

Big dark clouds were puffing on the horizon, the scent of rain was in the air, and yes, the wind was pushing us. I opened the box and saw a cheap plastic container inside, wrapped in a clear plastic bag. Feeling a little queasy, I set the box and bag in the back of the Explorer then carried the plastic container back to the grave. With Mama chain-smoking and wiping her eyes, and a storm coming, I didn't know what ceremonial words to speak, and whatever I said, I needed to hurry.

"I'm sorry there's not much to talk about," I

said aloud to Great Aunt Nola. "And I'm sorry you had to travel so much before you got here. Now go rest your soul and leave us alone."

I squatted down and pried the container open. The wind whooshed gray ash into the air. I jumped back, barely avoiding a face full of Great Aunt Nola. "Don't get her in your eyes," Mama yelled. Rain began to spatter us. I quickly spread the feathery pile of ashes across the graves, then rushed to the Explorer and thrust the empty container into the plastic bag. My hands and face felt dusty. My stomach rolled.

"There was a Taco Bell just off the highway," Mama said.

I drove quickly.

In the restroom of that fast-food restaurant I washed some small fraction of Great Aunt Nola down the sink. I rinsed and soaped and rinsed again—hands, face, neck, face, again. My duty to Grandma and my Daddyside great aunts had been fulfilled, but they'd always be with me, under my skin where I couldn't wash them away, and probably didn't want to, anyway.

When I came out of the bathroom, Mama handed me two soft drinks and a bag of burritos. "Go get us a table," she said. "I'll take care of the rest." Then she went out to the car with the rain peppering her, got the box and the bag and the dusty, empty plastic urn, and I watched through the restaurant's giant, wet plate-glass windows as she stuffed everything in an outside trash container. She flashed me a satisfied smile as she came back inside, then she hurried into the bathroom. She came out a few minutes later with her hands and face scrubbed pink, like mine.

I could manage a wan smile of my own, now.

"Let's eat," I said.

Although thunder boomed around us so hard that the restaurant windows shook, we ate our burritos in contented silence. I had Mama, and Mamaside was finally free of Daddyside. Finally peaceful. Outside, the wind moved in great, long gusts, picking up God-alone-knew what, or who, in its path.

Great Aunt Nola was still traveling.

GRANDMA TELLS A TALE

By Donna Ball

*The literature of women's lives is a tradition of escapees,
women who have lived to tell the tale...They resist captivity.
They get up and go. They seek better worlds.*
—Phyllis Rose

Story telling is endemic in my family. My earliest memories involve sitting on Great-grandmama Minnie's knee—she of the black widow's bonnet and cracked leather lace-up boots and gnarled spotted hands—and being mesmerized to an absolutely luscious terror by such gruesome rural legends as "The Snake in the Cabbage Patch"and "Red Eyes" while my mother argued, perhaps not as firmly as she could have, that those kinds of stories were probably not fit for a child my age before bedtime.

On that she was wrong. Stories of any kind were good for me, any time of the day or night. I hungered for them, thrived on them, relished every syllable with big-eyed anticipation. There is an atavistic connection between children and storytelling that has been handed down from the cave. And in my family, it has always been a way of life.

Grandma Hilda, though, has never been known as a raconteur. Her stories tend to be pointless, long-winded, rambling, outrageous and just plain disappointing. If it's a joke, she forgets the punch line. If it's a parable, she leaves out the axiom. If it's historical, she often gets the main characters wrong. It's common for her to spend five or ten minutes building the background for what she assures us will be a great story, then interrupt herself with "Ya'll know Jess Williams, don't you, Sarah Williams' boy?"

No, Grandma, we say, we don't know him. But that doesn't matter, you go ahead.

"But I could've sworn you knew him."

We assure her we do not, but want to hear the story anyway.

"No," she sighs, disappointed. "It won't mean anything if you don't know him."

Whereupon, likely as not, she'll launch into another tale just as probable to remain forever unfinished. The story-telling gene, I learned early on, was not dominant on Grandma Hilda's side of the family.

That is not to say that many an entertaining tale has not been told about her. For example, she's the one who, while chatting on the phone one morning with her sister, Montene, suddenly smelled the odor of burning food.

"Montene," she exclaimed, worried. " Have you got something on the stove?"

Montene, on the other end of the line fifteen miles away, allowed that she did not.

"Well, I smell something burning. Are you sure you're not cooking beans?"

Montene replied irritably, "Well, I'm sitting right here in the kitchen, and I guess I'd know if I had something on the stove. It must be on your end."

As you can see, it was eccentricity, more than anything else, that ran in Grandma Hilda's family.

She was known for interrupting conversations in the middle of a sentence to relate a long and involved piece of gossip about someone no one in the room knew; for making inappropriate comments about other people's weight, hairstyle, clothing and, yes, odor; for asking questions and walking out of the room before hearing the answer. She was never the most popular guest at family gatherings.

The first time Grandma Hilda met my daughter's fiancé, she looked him up and down and declared mildly, "Why, he looks just like that fellow on that television show. Killed three women, didn't he? Raped them too. Lord, child, how did you ever meet such a man?"

It took us the rest of the evening to persuade her that my future son-in-law had not last been seen on *America's Most Wanted*, and I still was not entirely sure she believed that Jill was not marrying a serial killer. As for Jill's husband, we knew he was marriage material when he learned to take Grandma Hilda in stride.

Though she was an embarrassment and an annoyance, though friends and family members had developed an attitude of pained resignation when it came to Grandma Hilda, it also has to be said that she was among the most generous people I have ever known. My brother and I will always remember her as the bearer of three-foot tall stuffed Easter bunnies and giant, chocolate-filled baskets wrapped in purple and yellow cellophane, of electric train sets and talking dolls at Christmas time, of birthday presents that included portable televisions and tape recorders.

Grandma Hilda gave me my first grown-up piece of jewelry, a diamond chip-studded dinner ring that was far too extravagant for a girl of twelve, but which I treasure to this day. From the time she was born, my daughter was showered with toys, clothing and lavish and oftentimes age-inappropriate gifts of all kinds—a ten speed bike before she was five, roller skates when she was twenty-two—and for a wedding gift, Grandma Hilda presented the bridal couple with a car. That the car was twenty-five years old and leaked oil like a sieve was of little consequence; as always, with Grandma Hilda, it was the thought that counted.

She wasn't a rich woman; she lived in the same farm house in which my mother had grown up, on a modest insurance policy my grandfather had left and her retirement from thirty years at the shirt factory. But she liked to give presents. And although her gifts grew in eccentricity as she did (one Christmas, for example, I received a day planner from the previous year—with the appointments already filled in), and although we knew the chances were high that whatever we gave her for her birthday would be returned to us, beautifully wrapped and presented as new, for Christmas, she still, on occasion, would surprise us. The Christmas of 1995 was just such a surprise.

This was Jill's first Christmas as a new bride, and she had agreed to spend it with her husband's family in Michigan. I imagine the fact that it was Grandma Hilda's turn to host the holiday dinner played a significant part in Jill's decision.

Braced for disaster, for dinner at Grandma Hilda's could result in anything from the firing of the preacher (Easter, 1982), to fist fights (summer, 1985), to food poisoning (Thanksgiving, 1990), my brother, my mother and I dressed ourselves up, armed ourselves with festively wrapped gifts, and presented ourselves at Grandma Hilda's red-foil-covered door at precisely twelve noon.

It was one of the most pleasant Christmases I can recall. The table was set with vintage linens and the silver polished to within an inch of its life. A platter of sliced turkey and ham was accompanied by homemade cranberry relish, a variety of green and yellow vegetables, and yeast rolls that had been rising since six a.m. When she put her mind to it and read the labels, my Grandma Hilda could out-cook Julia Child.

A fire was lit in the seldom-used parlor with its moth-eaten burgundy velvet curtains and mantelpiece supported by white-lacquered Corinthian columns. In one corner stood a small Christmas tree that was decorated with tinsel and old-fashioned red and green glass balls. We took our coffee and cake—an exquisite coconut so light it practically melted on the fork—into the parlor to exchange gifts.

From Grandma Hilda my mother received a blender, as I recall, a very nice model with a food processor attachment that she had been wanting. My brother and I opened identical-sized packages, each one containing a beautifully stitched and brightly patterned cotton quilt. Another package just like ours awaited delivery to Jill.

"Now I want y'all to take good care of those," admonished Grandma Hilda somberly. "I worked all year putting them together. Had to take a class to learn how to do it. My eyes are getting so bad I knew this would probably be the last chance I got to do fine work, and I wanted to leave you children something to remember me by."

My brother, my mother and I exchanged astonished glances. To the best of our knowledge, Grandma Hilda—although she had many other laudable skills—had never picked up a needle in her life. And yet, within a year she had taken a quilting class and had designed and put together not one but three truly beautiful quilts.

We smoothed the folds of the fabric reverently and carefully rearranged the tissue around our treasures. We assured her that our gifts were beyond anything we could have ever expected and would become cherished family heirlooms for generations.

Pleased, she settled back in her fireside wing chair, crossed plump ankles beneath the hem of her silk print skirt, and folded her hands in her lap in best finishing-school style. It was clear the best was yet to come.

"Now," she announced, "do you want to hear my Christmas story?"

This time the glances we exchanged were slightly uneasy. But the day had been exceptionally pleasant so far, and we were game for anything.

"Sure," volunteered my brother, trying to sound enthusiastic.

"Can't wait," I agreed.

My mother looked at her watch doubtfully. "We need to get on the road before too much longer."

Grandma Hilda cleared her throat and began. "This happened way back in 1933," she said, "when your mama was just a baby. Now this was during the depression and times were hard. We didn't know if we'd have Christmas dinner on the table, much less money for presents. I took in laundry to try to make a little extra for Christmas, and your granddaddy, God rest him, was working overtime down at the lumber mill.

"It was Christmas Eve, and I got up before dawn to make your granddaddy's breakfast and send him off to work. He told me he was only going to work a half day, then stop in town before the stores closed to bring home a few little things for Laura Lee's first Christmas.

"All we had back then was a wood stove to cook on and keep warm by, and I used to keep the cradle right there by the stove while I worked, ironing and cooking. Long about the middle of the morning I went out to get some more wood but the wood box was empty. Your granddaddy had been working so hard he'd forgotten to fill it. So I went out to the shed and got the ax, and took it down to the wood-pile to split some wood for the rest of the day. It was cold, too, and looking like it was going to commence to snow. You know, it was a lot colder back then than it is now. We used to have snow quite a bit."

I confess at this point I let my mind wander, anticipating another one of Grandma Hilda's long digressions. But, as though sensing her audience's fading attention, she returned to the point almost immediately.

"While I was out there, cutting wood, I heard a car coming up the driveway and when I looked it was the sheriff in his big old Pontiac. Now I'd been doing some ironing for his wife, who'd been feeling poorly all winter, and I figured that was what he'd come by about. I told him I'd bring the ironing over a little later, and he said he didn't want me to bother, that they'd come by and get it after Christmas. Said there was an escaped convict on the loose, and I was to be sure and keep my doors locked until your granddaddy got home. This fellow was a murderer, he said, chopped up a whole family up in Jackson County with an ax last year. I told him not to worry, that it being Christmas Eve your granddaddy would be home early. But I'd be careful just the same.

"Well, he'd no sooner gone back down the driveway than I heard Laura Lee crying, so I just stuck the ax in the tree stump, gathered me up an armload of wood, and hurried back to the house. By the time I got her fed and changed it was starting to snow, and it was about time for your granddaddy to come home. It was starting to come on dark, so I went around the house lighting lanterns. When I got to the parlor here, I happened to look out that window over yonder..."

We all instinctively turned our heads toward the window she indicated.

"And Lord, if I didn't see a man staring back at me!"

She said it with such drama that I actually caught my breath, half-expecting to see a face appear in the window at which I was staring.

"He was a mean-looking thing, too, with a beard and wild tangled hair, and standing there with snow on his clothes in his shirt sleeves. And then I saw him start to move across the porch, you know, over to the front door, and it wasn't until then that I remembered what the sheriff had said. I ran to the front door and locked it not two seconds before he started rattling the door handle.

"Then I remembered the baby sleeping back in

the kitchen by the fire—with the back door unlocked. I ran through the house, threw the bolt on the back door and snatched up my little girl, and I blew out the lantern and hunched up against the wall, scared to death."

We were riveted. My brother made sounds of amazement and disbelief, and even my mother was wide-eyed. I urged, "What happened?"

I have never seen a woman so skillfully hold an audience in her hand as did my Grandma Hilda on that occasion. "Well," she continued, with an obvious relish of every word, "the longest time passed, and I figured whoever it was had just gone on. You know it was the Depression and we weren't that far from the railroad. Used to get a lot of hobos and bums coming to the back door. I started to feel kind of silly, and bad that I'd locked the door like that on Christmas Eve."

A product of our own times, we all exclaimed that she had done exactly the right thing, for who knew what might have happened if she hadn't locked the door?

Grandma Hilda nodded. "It was getting on late, though, and I was starting to worry about your granddaddy. The roads were slippery and that old truck of ours didn't work half the time, and what if there was a killer out there? We didn't have a phone, and even if we did I wouldn't know who to call. In another hour or so it would be dark, and if your granddaddy was in a ditch somewhere he'd freeze to death before morning.

"We had an old mule, and a surrey that we'd drive to church sometimes when the weather was fair. I knew I was going to have to hitch up that mule and go off looking for my husband myself, or at least ride down the road to the sheriff's house, and take him away from his wife on Christmas Eve to go out hunting for him. So I went out to the barn, with the snow coming down so hard I couldn't hardly keep it out of my eyes, and left the baby sleeping by the stove in the house."

Oh, we knew something bad was coming. Obviously the baby—my mother—had survived the ordeal, whatever it had been, and so had my grandmother. But we were tense and breathless just the same. Like spectators at a silent movie who had thrown ripe fruit at the villain on the screen, we wanted to shout, "Don't go in the barn! Don't leave the baby alone!"

Grandma Hilda went on, "I got about half way across the yard when I saw him again—that man who'd been at the window. He was slipping around the porch toward the back. I guess he'd been hiding in the barn all afternoon, and when I came out, he took his chance to get in the house. But I'd left baby Laura Lee in there, all alone.

"Then I remembered how I'd stuck the ax in the stump that afternoon when I finished cutting wood. I ran across the yard toward the wood pile, but the ax was gone! That man had it, and he was in the house with my baby!"

"Good heavens," I exclaimed, when I couldn't stand the dramatic pause any longer. "What in the world did you do?"

Grandma Hilda swept the room with a thoughtful gaze, assessing the mood. It must have been satisfactory, because she continued, "I snuck into the house, that's what. I crept around the back porch and I pushed open the kitchen door, and I could hear him moving around in there, with the floorboards creaking and all. But Laura Lee was still sleeping in her cradle by the stove, so I snatched her up and I ran out into the snow.

"I hadn't even put on a coat when I went out, and all I had to keep the snow off the baby was my apron. You know our skirts were real long then, and I kept tripping over mine. I ran down the driveway and down to the road, and it felt like nearly a mile in the snow and the dark. And who should I meet on the road but the sheriff and his deputy? Seems like they'd tracked that old convict to my house and thought I was in there with him, killed or hostage. They were coming to rescue me!"

"Did they catch him?" my brother wanted to know.

"Oh, they caught him, all right. Right here in the house. Shot him in the shoulder and dragged him back off to state prison."

"What about Daddy?" my mother wanted to know. "Where was he?"

"Just like I thought, off in a ditch. But a neighbor had seen the tire tracks and pulled him out, and he was already on his way home. He'd gotten a bonus from the lumber yard, and he brought home a country ham, and a china doll for you and a quilted bathrobe for me. We had the best Christmas ever."

An awed and appreciative silence fell at the conclusion of her tale. We all three looked at each other, and I pronounced the collective opinion. "That," I said, "was the best story I've ever heard."

We bombarded her with questions. How had he escaped? Who was he? Did he really have the ax?

44

Wasn't she scared to death? Why had we never heard this story before?

"Because," she answered, so pleased with herself she was practically beaming, "I was saving it. This is your Christmas present."

We all agreed that, as presents go, she had outdone herself.

When Jill got home from Michigan two days later, I couldn't wait to tell her what she'd missed. A peaceful, non-toxic dinner, hand-made Christmas gifts, and the most riveting after-dinner Christmas story I had ever heard—one that was not only a thrilling and heretofore unknown episode in our family history, but one that was actually told coherently from beginning to end. And told by Grandma Hilda. Excitedly, I began to repeat the tale.

I got to the part where Grandma Hilda went to the barn and saw the man sneaking around the back when Jill interrupted me.

"And then she looked over at where she'd left the ax, and it was gone."

I stared at her.

"And then," continued Jill, "she sneaked back into the house and grabbed up the baby and ran out into the snow and met the sheriff on the road, right?"

I frowned, disappointed. "How did you know? When did she tell you this story?"

Jill burst into laughter. "I don't believe it! Mama, she didn't tell it to me! It was the movie of the week last Sunday!"

❋❋❋

That was our last Christmas with Grandma Hilda. She passed away quietly in her sleep the following July at the age of eighty-six. The next autumn as I was airing out the winter linens I came across the box with the heirloom quilt in it, still carefully wrapped in tissue to preserve it for future generations. Impulsively, I took it out and spread it on my bed. As I did, the corner flipped down and a white tag was plainly visible on the underside. It said: Made in Japan.

I sat down on the bed, and I laughed. And then I cried.

I cried for giant Easter rabbits and extravagant birthday cards, for funny stories about an eccentric lady who always did things her way, and who was, without a doubt, one of a kind. I remembered her last, best gift, and my laughter was a tribute to the woman who had, in the end, outdone us all: she told a story and made our eyes grow big with wonder; she presented us with quilts and made us marvel at their beauty; she made us happy, and she pleased herself.

As always with Grandma Hilda, it was the thought that counted.

KEEPER OF THE STICK

By Virginia Ellis

*Grown-ups never understand anything for themselves, and it's
tiresome for children to be forever explaining things to them.
—Antoine de St. Exupery*

My daddy was a trucker, and he mostly hauled cattle. That means that four-legged critters are involved in most of the memories from my childhood. Believe me, if you've ever slipped and fallen in a warm, newly-dropped cow patty, the image stays with you for life.

One of my first cow memories comes from when I was around four and half years old. I know my age because of the events that took place. That day, like many others, my daddy had a load of cattle to move. No cattle, no money. It was a concept even a four-year-old could understand.

Unfortunately, when he arrived with his truck, the cattle weren't in a pen. They were loose in a fifty acre pasture and so far away that you could barely see them in the distance. My daddy and the farmer who owned the cows spent all day on foot trying to herd the cattle into the loading pen. The man had shaken his head and explained that these particular cattle hadn't seen a person in several years so they were a little spooky.

So not only were the cattle not where they were supposed to be, they were "wild" cattle. In more recent times it's been said that you can't "tune a fish." Well, I'm sorry to report to all you animal lovers out there, in my experience you can't do much with a cow either—except chase 'em.

And that's what my daddy did, until almost dark. As a last resort, and I know this to be true because my momma was around eight and a half months into the manufacture of my little sister, my daddy came home to get her, my older sister, and me to help load the cows. No cows, no money.

All we needed, he explained, was a few more unfamiliar bodies in the way to keep the cows from splitting up and heading for the back of the pasture. So not long after that, I found myself standing in the fading afternoon light near Daddy's eighteen-wheeler with a stick in my hand. My job, because I was the smallest, was to stand beyond the gate of the pen and keep the cows from running right past it. Daddy explained that these cows were scared of humans and that if I waved that stick, they'd turn the other way.

All I had to do was stand there.

It sounded reasonable to me, although I didn't like the idea of being the only one left behind when the rest went out in the pasture to herd the cattle. They were gone a long time. I spent what felt like hours practicing with my stick and staring off into the growing twilight until finally I saw them coming. I could see my dad first, he was the tallest, then my mom walking and waving a towel, then I saw the cows. My heart started pounding. I never even looked for my older sister.

My eyes were locked on what were undoubtedly the biggest cows I'd ever seen. And they didn't look too happy about going anywhere with my daddy.

Now that I'm older I can say I was probably facing twenty full-grown cattle with a few calves. In my four-year-old memory, however, there were at least a hundred of them racing out of the darkness, and they were wild-eyed.

I could hear my daddy give a shrill whistle every once in a while and a few of the cows would jump forward. I walked out, away from the safety of the truck, and held up my stick. My brain knew what I had to do and kept repeating my daddy's words: Just stand there.

But it was like my feet had eyes. They could see those cattle, and they didn't want to be the only spindly thing between wild cattle and escape. I'd never felt so small in my short life, and my cowardly feet took two steps closer to the truck.

The nearer the cows got, the more agitated they became. If they hadn't seen humans in awhile, they certainly hadn't seen an eighteen-wheeler or a four-year-old with a stick. What if they didn't know enough to be afraid of me? I took another two steps closer to the truck and waved the stick.

That's when things went south.

The cattle seemed to sense that this might be their last trip in life and, instead of going into the pen, they bolted. I heard my daddy yell for me to chase them back.

But that's when the problem with my feet became acute. After one frozen, horrified gaze at the "thundering herd," I dropped the stick and ran for the truck, pulling myself onto the step-up as the cattle went by.

I was alive, but totally humiliated. Everybody was standing there tired and frustrated, looking at me, and I felt like I'd failed the only mission I'd been given in life. If I remember, my daddy asked what happened. I wanted to say that someone taller should have been in charge of the stick. But instead, I confessed that I'd been too scared, and my sister called me a scaredy cat. Then my mom just gave me a hug and said, "It's okay."

The farmer, I guess with some remorse about my daddy chasing his crazy cows all day, said he figured we'd done all we could do. He'd find someone to come in the morning with horses to herd the cows into the pen. Then he did something amazing. He opened his wallet and gave my dad ten dollars to buy us some dinner since we'd missed it fooling with his cows.

Not only did we have dinner, which I remember as being the most wonderful ham sandwich I'd ever eaten, (we didn't eat in restaurants much) but we also went to the drive-in. I don't recall what the movie was. Near the end of it, however, my momma started feeling bad and we had to go home. When I woke up the next morning, my grandma was at the house and she said we had a new baby sister.

Now a four-year-old's mind can ramble in some odd directions. I used to wonder if those cows had scared my little sister right out of my momma's belly like they'd scared me up onto Daddy's truck, and I watched to see if that fright might have a lasting affect on her. But she grew up normal, didn't become a cow-hater or a vegetarian. I've never seen her actually interact with a cow—most of her adventures were with horses—so I guess we all made it through the cow chase unscathed.

As for my daddy, he hauled cattle for a few more years and gave me a few more tales to tell before he switched to gasoline. You don't have to herd gasoline, unless it catches on fire. But, that's another story...

❖❖❖

Author's note: After writing this story, I sent the manuscript to my mother thinking she would get a kick out of it. I called her a few days later and asked how she'd liked it. Of course, she said it was wonderful and that she couldn't believe I had remembered so much at such a young age.

As I was congratulating myself on a job well-done, she continued talking. "There's just one thing," she said.

I thought maybe I'd missed some small detail since she'd already congratulated me on doing a fine job, so I wasn't nervous.

"Uh—" She seemed reluctant to speak.

"Well, what did I forget?" I asked.

"We got the cows," she answered. "That's why the farmer gave us money for dinner. And as far as I remember, you didn't run," my mother said. "You might have moved, but you didn't run. Everything else is just as it happened."

Now herein lies the lesson, not only for writers but for children everywhere. All I can figure is, at four and a half I wanted to run so bad that in my memory, I had. In my memory I was the goat who had failed the test when in real life I had stood there, albeit moving slightly, and did my job.

I am making a promise to myself right now, and forever more, to remember being the best I could be in any situation.

'Cause sometimes, I was.

51

FINGERPRINTS

by Donna Ball

*[Tradition] cannot be inherited, and if you want it
you must obtain it by great labour.*
—T.S. Eliot

W hat most people don't understand about
the Southern family is how deeply our
roots are planted in the subsoil of the
past. Nourished by ritual and fortified by necessity,
our strength lies in the blood of all the generations
who have gone before us. Scratch any Southern family and you'll find a story of a young boy who fought
a wild cat with a pocket knife, a mother who hid her
children in a well to protect them from marauders, a
husband who crossed a mountain barefoot to bring
nourishment to his starving family. These are not heroes, they are not legends. They are simply men and
women who did what had to be done. Like the faded
daguerreotypes that hang from the walls of weather-
beaten home places across the South, they are our
heritage.

Opening weekend of bird season had been a
tradition in my husband's family for as long as anyone could remember. All the boys would gather, driv-

ing in from wherever in the state they happened to be on Friday night after work, back to the old home place. There would be a big pot of chicken and dumplings on the back burner of the stove, ready to be ladled up as the children and grandchildren came in, with fried fruit pies for dessert. There was milk in a fat blue ceramic pitcher for the children, and black coffee for the adults. The women would feed the children and catch up on the gossip while the men sat around a coal-burning stove, telling tall tales and oiling down their hunting boots with melted lard to protect them from the cold dew and wet bogs of the morning's hunt. The aromas of gun oil and hot coffee, simmering chicken and hard-working men combined into a thick sensory stew that, even now, can take me back in an instant to a time and a place that will never come again.

Miss Jewel and Mr. Bill—who were never called anything else by anyone except their own children—produced four living boys, of whom my husband was the oldest. All the boys were raised on the bounty of the land, fishing with cane poles in lazy summer ponds, tramping through frosty fields in search of deer or quail in the winter, but not ashamed to bring home a squirrel or rabbit for the stew pot when that was all they could find. What they killed, they ate. What they raised in the fields, they prepared or preserved.

Miss Jewel still collected eggs from her own chickens every morning, and twice a day brought in milk warm from the cow. Mr. Bill held a hog-killing once a year, and salted and smoked his own meat. Once, as a very new bride, I inquired why in the world they would want to go to so much trouble when the supermarket three miles down the road could sell eggs, meat and milk for far less than it cost my in-laws to shelter and feed the animals that produced the same. My naivete was met with first a blank look, then with a tolerant, "Because that's the way it's done, sugar. "

That's the way it's done.

Their sons had grown rather far away from their roots over the years, going off to the suburbs to work in factories or start their own businesses or, in the case of Little Earl (so named after Mr. Bill's brother, who had died a hero in WWII)to teach high school. They came home for Christmas and Thanksgivings and birthdays, and on weekends when they could. But once a year they came home to their past, took up their shotguns and donned their caps and hunting vests, and did things the way they had always been done.

No one saw any reason that things should be different the year Mr. Bill had his stroke.

Not that there hadn't been some discussion. The stroke had left the family patriarch weak on his left side and occasionally forgetful, a shrunken memory of his former robust self who moved like an old man and whose blue eyes were sometimes, terrifyingly, confused. It was painful to watch; heart wrenching to think about. Here was a man we thought would never die. But plainly he was more mortal than any of us wanted to admit.

There were hasty telephone calls between the sisters-in-law, worried debate between the brothers, and, finally, a direct confrontation with Miss Jewel herself. Surely she wasn't going to let Mr. Bill go hunting this year. Was he strong enough? What did the doctor say? Wouldn't it be best to just skip the whole thing until he was stronger?

But that stoic woman, with pain in her eyes and a grim set to her mouth, only replied that it wasn't her place to tell Mr. Bill what he could or couldn't do, and Mr. Bill was determined to go hunting on opening weekend, just the way he always had. She would expect to see us all on Friday night.

The way she said it let us know that the subject had been raised in heated debate between her husband and herself on more than one occasion. Of course she didn't want him to go. And of course he didn't want things to change. In the end I think it wasn't so much Mr. Bill's stubborness that won out, as it was Miss Jewel's compassion—and perhaps the compassion of all of us. I guess we all knew that if we waited for Mr. Bill to get stronger, there would never be another Opening Weekend hunt. And so the tradition would continue this year as it had every other one—for him. For all of us.

Little Earl had married a city girl six months previously, and this would be her first weekend with her husband's family. It was obvious from the moment Cathy walked in the door, wearing a pale blue wool coat and matching pillbox hat, clutching an envelope bag in died-to-match blue and smiling a smile that looked as though it might crack her cheeks at any moment, that Miss Jewel and Mr. Bill weren't the only ones who had had words about the weekend. I felt sorry for her up until the moment she swept a distressed glance from the stew pot on the cook stove to the men who were dipping old rags into the soup can of melted lard on the coal stove, wrinkled her nose and inquired, "What is that *smell*?"

Behind her, carrying the three pieces of monogrammed luggage that Cathy's parents had given them for a wedding gift, Little Earl smiled wanly and apologetically, and we all returned looks of sympathy.

We bedded down early– children sharing featherbeds and mounds of quilts with their parents in the unheated upstairs rooms where the temperatures hovered around freezing on cold November mornings— and were up long before first light. Miss Jewel started stirring at four o'clock, shuffling downstairs to mix up yeast biscuits in a big blue bowl and set it to rise on the back of the stove, opening the creaky pantry door and slicing country ham from the shoulder that hung there, heating an iron skillet, filling the percolator with water. I snuggled deeper into the downy bed, letting the familiar sounds paint comforting memory pictures for me, while my husband stretched and yawned and muttered about how no bird was worth getting up this early for, just like he did every year. And then we were both silent, listening and not wanting to listen to the not so pleasant sounds that were coming from Cathy and Little Earl's room across the hall.

Words like "stupid" and "barbaric" shot sharply through the tempered oak boards that separated the rooms. "You hate hunting!" Cathy cried. "You told me so yourself!"

"I do not hate it. Lower your voice."

My husband and I looked at each other in the dark. Everyone knew Little Earl was not the best hunter in the family. The fact that he went on these trips out of a sense of duty rather than genuine enjoyment of the sport was no secret to anyone—except perhaps Mr. Bill. Would this be the year he backed out of the expedition? Would he let his father down?

"And you're taking that sick old man with you, making him carry a gun! What kind of son are you?

What if something happens out there? Are all you all crazy?"

"Nothing's going to happen." Little Earl's voice sounded tired, as though he'd had the argument many times before.

"And what about me?" She was tearful now. "You're just going to leave me here all alone, worrying myself to death about whether you ever come back..."

"Cathy, I'm coming back."

"Well maybe you shouldn't! Maybe if you care more about—about killing things with a gun than you do about me, well maybe you should just stay out there in the woods with your brothers and your gun!"

"Cathy, honey..."

She burst into sobs, and I was embarrassed on behalf of all womankind.

It was an uncomfortable group that trooped down to breakfast at 5:30 that morning, all of us rubbing our hands and putting on our happy faces, keeping our voices low so as not to wake the children and trying, by turn, not to look at either Cathy and Little Earl or Miss Jewel and Mr. Bill. Wordlessly, Miss Jewel poured black cups of coffee and served up big platters of country fried ham and eggs, buttery grits and soft hot biscuits with hand-pressed butter and four kinds of jam. Mr. Bill's shaking hand scattered sugar all over the checked vinyl tablecloth and we all pretended not to notice. Cathy kept her head low and pushed her food around on her plate with her fork, and we pretended not to notice.

The men bolted down their meal and drained the dregs of the coffee. They pushed ammunition into the loop holders on their vests, they lowered the ear flaps on their caps, they shouldered their shotguns. They kissed their wives. Little Earl's kiss, I noticed, was stiff and reserved, and Cathy clung to his sleeve for a moment, looking into his eyes, before abruptly turning away. Mr. Bill pinched Miss Jewel's cheek, like he always did, and told her to keep a pot of coffee on the stove. He liked it hot and strong, he told her, like his women. We all laughed at that, like we always did, everyone except Miss Jewel. But the laughter was strained, and faded as we watched him shuffle down the steps, holding on tight to the rail while his sons hovered anxiously around him.

We stood at the screen door and watched them walk down the dirt drive away from the house, the bird dogs barking and bouncing excitedly alongside them. Our menfolk, going off to conquer the world on our behalf, just as they had done since time immemorial. Strong and young, old and weak, as different as five men could be but united by brotherhood, they were for that moment as close to a single unit as it was possible to be.

It was foggy out, and barely light, and our noble hunters were swallowed up by the gloom after a dozen or so steps. Still, we stood there in the cold and the damp, watching. Then Miss Jewel said flatly, "Dang fool. Even if he could see the bird, he couldn't lift the gun to shoot it."

She closed the door firmly, and we turned back into the kitchen to begin our chores.

It soon became apparent that Cathy was about as useful in a kitchen as a rubber corkscrew. After she had broken two of Miss Jewel's coffee cups, put the butter dish on the back of the stove instead of in the refrigerator—where it promptly dissolved into a puddle of cream—and fed the cat out of a Haviland saucer, we sent her out with the children to gather pecans.

"Poor Little Earl," said Miss Jewel sadly, setting the misused cat's saucer in a pan of ammonia to soak. "Remind me to make him up a box of canned goods before they leave."

There were two big pecan trees that shaded the house, and most years provided us with an abundance of nuts for our holiday pies, cookies and cakes. Traditionally it was the youngsters' jobs—and this year we had a collection ranging from ages three to eight—to gather and shell the pecans while we women readied the kitchen for the annual baking of the fruitcakes. For as long as the men had been leaving their wives at home alone on the opening day of bird season, the women had been using the time to make our batch of Six-Week Fruitcakes. And since the prime ingredient in the famous fruitcake was, in fact, eighty-proof, it was generally a very festive time.

All morning we worked, getting a meal on the stove for when our hungry men came tramping in after midday, full of swagger and tales of triumph. Occasionally we would hear the barking of a dog or the report of a shotgun, and we would look at each other, our eyes reflecting worry and relief—worry because the sound of a gunshot was by its nature disturbing, but relieved because at least it meant they were still close by. We fried up a pan of chicken and one of ham, filled an iron skillet with buttermilk cornbread and rolled out a pan of biscuits. We put a couple of pots of vegetables on the stove to simmer with salt pork.

All the while we gossiped, catching up on the

news since we had all seen each other last, trying to keep Miss Jewel's mind off the only man she had ever loved, who was wandering around in the woods in a weakened condition with a loaded shotgun. I don't think one of us missed Cathy, or thought about her out there in the cold picking up pecans with the children. If she crossed our minds at all, it was in relief to have her out of the way.

At noon Cathy and the children came in, all of them red cheeked and chap-handed, lugging a bushel basket half filled with pecans between them. The children were laughing and excited, and even Cathy seemed pleased with her labors. No one had the heart to point out that half the nuts were unusable, having been tossed down by squirrels while they were still in their green husks.

When the children were fed and put down for their naps, the real work began. We still had a couple of hours before the men were expected back, and we wanted to at least have the cakes in the oven by then. For the second time that day we scrubbed the kitchen floor to ceiling, washed the dishes and carefully replaced them in the corner china cabinet, and stripped off the vinyl tablecloth. We spread newspapers over the long trestle table, and brought out the tube pans and the waxed paper. During most of this Cathy simply stood by looking helpless, so I sat her down at one end of the table and showed her how to cut out waxed paper liners for the pans. It was tedious work, and she looked less than thrilled.

Within moments the kitchen was filled with the fragrance of cloves and cinnamon and the tabletop transformed into a jeweled wonderland as small plastic tubs of candied citrus, cherries and chopped mixed fruit were emptied into piles. But it wasn't until Miss Jewel brought out a cider jug that had been filled with this year's chosen libation, muscadine wine, that we all let out a collective "aaahhh" of appreciation.

Miss Jewel ceremoniously poured each of us a thimbleful into a sherry glass–for purposes of tasting, you understand, and deciding whether the wine was fit to soak the fruitcakes in. We waited until everyone was served, we sniffed, we smiled, we tasted. We gave murmurs of delighted appreciation as the fresh heady taste of new wine warmed our mouths and our fingertips.

Cathy said, staring dubiously into her glass, "Are you sure it's safe to drink?"

"Unless you're a Baptist!" replied one of the sisters-in-law, and we all shrieked with laughter.

"It's smells kind of... sour," Cathy said, still looking at the glass as though she'd rather drink rat poison.

Miss Jewel went over to her, took her glass, sniffed it sharply, and drank the contents down. "Nope,"she pronounced, setting the glass down on the table with a clank. "Tastes fine to me."

We grinned, and emptied our glasses.

Miss Jewel traditionally chose one assistant to work with her, sifting flour and beating eggs, while she mixed up the thick rich batter that was the basis for the fruitcake, while the rest of us chopped fruit and nuts and prepared the pans. It was only right that this year she choose Cathy, the newest member of the family.

We were making a half dozen cakes, one for each family and one to give away, and the bowl we used was approximately the size of a washtub. We held our collective breath when Cathy picked up the bowl, half-filled with fruitcake batter, and transferred it from the mixer stand to the counter top, where the last of the sifted flour would be folded in by hand. But our relieved smiles and raised eyebrows were shared a moment too soon. Cathy picked up the paper towel—yes, paper—upon which she had sifted six cups of flour and the requisite spices, and turned to carry it to the bowl. Six cups of flour and spices rained down onto Miss Jewel's freshly mopped floor when the paper towel split.

I've got to say, we were all feeling a little sorry for Cathy by that point. She was such an obvious misfit, helpless in the kitchen, completely out of her element with her husband's family. But it was, after all, six cups of flour and the last of the cinnamon she had spilled, and no one could say for sure what shape the rest of the batter would be in by the time one of us drove to store for more supplies. Miss Jewel decided to take no chances, threw out the contents of the big bowl, and started over.

It was well after two o'clock by the time we all resumed our places at the big table. Cathy was assigned the relatively harmless job of separating the nut meats from the shell with a silver nut pick.. Miss Jewel stirred the batter in the big yellow bowl with a wooden spoon, the rest of us chopped candied fruit and rolled it in a mixture of flour and spice. We sipped daintily on our little glasses of muscadine wine while we worked, but the talk grew desultory as the afternoon wore on. We kept glancing toward the window, and trying not to. We hadn't heard a gunshot in a long time, nor the bark of a dog.

Finally Cathy burst out, "Where *are* they? Earl said they'd be home by lunch!"

We called the midday meal "dinner" in the country. Somehow, her simple misuse of a word separated her from us more than anything else she had done that day. We glanced at each other, but no one answered right away.

Then Miss Jewel said in a tone as calm and flat as though she were reporting the weather, "They'll be along directly."

"Probably walked over to Henry's Flat," someone offered.

"That's an awful long way," someone else worried.

"One of those fool dogs might've got loose."

"That's probably it."

Cathy's gaze darted from woman to woman as though each one might hold the answer to a prayer. I tried to make my smile reassuring as I told her, "They're never out later than four."

At four o'clock, I said, "They've got another good hour before dark. They'll be here."

But it had started to rain, a slow, ugly, bone-chilling drizzle, and I tried not to think what this weather might do to an already fragile old man. I tried not to look at Miss Jewel while I thought it.

The first batch of fruitcakes went into the oven and filled the house with the warm baking aroma of vanilla and spice. The children, tantalized by the fragrance, made pests of themselves underfoot until they were sent off to the parlor with cookies and milk and a trunkful of old clothes to play dress-up with. The light faded from the lowering gray sky while we chopped more fruit and nuts for the second batch of cakes, and Miss Jewel pulled the chain on the bare bulb that was suspended over the table. A pool of yellow light spilled over our busy fingers and made soft circles in our glasses of wine.

Suddenly Cathy cried out sharply and dropped the nut pick. A spot of blood appeared on her finger.

"What'd you do, prick yourself?"

"Let me see that, honey."

"Just rinse it off under the faucet, it's not bleeding much."

"I'll get a Band-aide."

"No," Miss Jewel said.

She pushed herself up from the table, wiped her hands on her gingham checked apron, and walked around to Cathy. "Come with me, child."

She led Cathy over to the mantle, took her bleeding finger, and pressed it firmly into the aged, stained oak of the mantlepiece. "There now," said Miss Jewel with satisfaction. "Now you go get yourself a bandage."

Cathy stared at her mother-in-law in a mixture of repulsion and horror. She looked at her bloody fingerprint on the mantle, which was already beginning to disappear into the oiled wood. She looked at us. We were smiling.

"You people," she said, quite distinctly, "are crazy."

She turned to leave the room, then whirled around again, her color high. "Your husbands are out there with guns! It's cold and wet and the grass is slippery... they could be lost or—or hurt—they're over two hours overdue and it's getting dark! Mr Bill shouldn't be out there at all and my Earl—he's never even *fired* a gun, did you know that? He hates guns!

You all think he's just like the rest of them and he lets you think it but he's never shot anything! But he couldn't let his daddy down, had to take him out on this stupid hunting trip... And instead of trying to stop them, you all sit here and bake fruitcakes and drink that horrid stuff you call wine and—and put blood on the mantelpiece! Why, that's not even sanitary! It's—it's crazy, you're all just crazy!"

Miss Jewel said, "Go wash you hands, honey, and come on back and finish them pecans. Smells to me like that first batch of cakes is about ready to come out."

Cathy looked from one to the other of us. Her voice was strained to the edge of cracking. "How can you sit there and not do anything? They could be hurt, or in trouble! How can you just sit there?"

The oven door creaked as Miss Jewel swung it open, and the sweet spice aroma was so thick we could almost see it. One by one, she removed the cakes from the oven with hands wrapped in dishtowels. And as she worked, she spoke.

"It was right after the War Between The States, and the County was plumb run over with Carpetbaggers and Reconstructionists. It was Willie Barber who built this house, you know, with his young bride Martha, before he went off to fight for the South. And he was one of the lucky ones who got to come back home.

"But what he came home to was a mess. Taxes sky high, law-breakers running the country, Yankees doing their best to beat down any good Southerner that tried to stand up for himself. I done some reading on that time; I know how it was. And that's why I believe this story.

"The year after the war, cash money was hard to come by. But somehow Willie Barber scraped together enough to pay the taxes on this place. He set off early in the morning to walk the twelve miles over to Jefferson, that was the county seat back then."

She turned the three tube pans upside down over Coke bottles to let them cool, and returned to the table, picking up her stirring spoon. She began to beat the flour mixture into the batter.

"He was long overdue, getting nigh on to dark, right like it is now, and Martha, I reckon she was getting mighty worried too. I can just see her face, and how relieved she must've been when she heard her man's footsteps on the stoop, and she ran to fling open the door– and he 'bout fell in on her, all covered with blood.

"Seems he'd been accosted in town, by a drunk with a knife, trying to steal his money. Willie fought back, and killed the man. Maybe it wouldn't've been so bad, but the drunk was a Yankee, and this Yankee was an important one—a commissioner or some such. Like I say, a man didn't have to have character to be runnin' things back then, and there were a lot of bad ones in charge.

"So anyways, there was Willie, cut bad on the arm and not too far ahead of the law, who wouldn't have much trouble proving him a killer, even if it was self-defense, if they found him there all bloody and beat up. The law was all Yankee law back then, and not inclined to hear a Southern boy's side of any story.

"Martha had to think fast. She hid Willie in the storm cellar, and mopped up the blood and dirt he'd trailed in so's there'd be no sign. When she heard the horses in the yard she knew they'd come for her man. She grabbed a kitchen knife and hid it in her apron pocket, just in case she had to do some fighting of her own that night. And then she stood right yonder in front of that mantlepiece and met those Yankee law officers just as cool as you please."

I scooped a double handful of chopped fruit into the batter Miss Jewel was stirring. So did my sister-in-law who sat next to her. Cathy sat with her hands in her lap, still and quiet-eyed, listening. Miss Jewel resumed speaking.

"No sir, she says, her husband wasn't in town today. No sir, she didn't know when he would be back. He'd gone off huntin' squirrel for the dinner table, she says, and he'd be back when he got back. No point in them waiting. Might as well move on.

"It might have worked, might not. But she saw it at the same time that Yankee lawman did—right there on the door, bigger than life, a bloody hand print. She thought she'd cleaned up all the blood, but she had missed that one place where her husband had leaned his hand. And it was enough to get him hung.

"'What this?' says the lawman, stooping down to get himself a better look. 'Looks like blood.'

"Martha, she feels that knife in her pocket, and she slides her hand down the handle, and onto the blade. And she closes her hand around it. Squeezes hard. 'It's mine,' she says, bringing out a hand smeared with blood. 'I cut myself when you knocked on the door. I didn't have a chance to wrap it.'"

I reached across the table, scooped up a cup of chopped nuts from Cathy's pile, and added them to the batter. Someone else tossed in several scoops of floured chopped dates. Miss Jewel stirred, the muscles in her small arms straining as she moved the batter back and forth.

"Now, you can't tell me," she went on, "that that lawman didn't know that wasn't Martha's blood on the door. He had to've known she'd just cut herself while he was standing there. But when one of his deputies got all riled and started talking about searching the house, so the story is told, he just stood there, looking at Martha, and he said, straight to her face, 'We don't doubt a lady's word, Mister. Her husband isn't here.'

"And they rode out from there and never came looking again. I reckon he figured a woman like that was nothing to be trifled with. Or maybe he was just glad to be shed of a bad apple, and grateful Willie had done the killing for him. But when they were gone, so the story's told, Martha was shaking so bad that she grabbed the mantle there, to keep herself upright, and left her bloody fingerprints. What with tending to Willie and worrying about the law, it was days before she thought about cleaning up, and by that time the blood stain had set into the wood. Reckon they could whitewash over the door, where Willie's handprint was, but not much you can do about that old knotty oak. Some say you can still see her fingerprints to this day, if you look real hard. I don't know, myself. Could be just the way old wood colors."

For a time there was no sound except the click of the spoon against the bowl and the faint patter of light rain against the tin roof, like tiny feet scurrying up above. Cathy's head was turned toward the mantle, and her eyes were oddly bright.

"It's been kind of a way with the women of this family," Miss Jewel went on after a time, "to add their fingerprints to Martha's on the mantlepiece there. Kind of reminds us who we are, and what we're made of. Must seem kinda silly to you, though, I reckon."

Cathy blinked, and swallowed, but didn't speak.

I said gently, "I'd been married two years before I felt like part of this family. Remember, Maddie? I cut my hand peeling potatoes and—"

"Lord, I thought it was the strangest thing I'd ever heard of. Like something Indians would do. But I took a sewing needle, myself and—"

One by one, we related our own stories of blood and struggle, and fingerprints left in wood. Crazy? Perhaps. But, like our men who had strode off into the dawn to observe a primal rite that no longer had any place in modern life, we too had our sacraments. They brought us home.

The clock on the mantle chimed six, and it was full dark. Silence fell, and we were acutely aware of how many ghosts our voices had been keeping at bay.

Cathy turned to look at us, her color mottled, her lashes wet. She swallowed hard. She said thickly, "What do you suppose Martha would have done tonight?"

We looked at each other. We listened to the rain and the darkness pressing against our small island of light. Then, without another word, we went to gather sweaters and flashlights, and we left the house in search of our men.

❋❋❋

We met them half way down the dirt road that led to the house, wet and cold but otherwise in good spirits. Mr. Bill was walking slowly, but beaming broadly, and his sons kept close and matched his pace.

"Got us a mess o' quail, old gal!" he called when our flashlights came into view. "Brought home supper one more time!"

Miss Jewel wrapped her arm around his and took the string of birds from his hands and she smiled, broadly and genuinely, for the first time that day.

When the weather started to go bad, it seems, they had taken shelter in the old fishing shack down by the pond, had a few sips of some moonshine Mr. Bill had hidden under a floorboard years ago, and had done some reminiscing of their own. We should have scolded them. But somehow it just didn't seem appropriate.

Little Earl hung back a little, as though uncertain of his welcome. He needn't have worried.

It was only after Cathy had disentangled herself from his arms that we all noticed he was carrying Mr. Bill's shotgun. A little shyly, he reached into the oversized pocket of his hunting jacket and brought out a brace of quail. "Pa let me shoot his gun," he said. There was uncertainty in his voice, and his eyes, as he searched his bride's face in the reflection of our flashlights, but there was also an unmistakable pride. "I got these two dead on, one shot each."

We were all silent, watching Cathy's reaction as her husband held the two bloodied birds before her. Little Earl hesitated, and started to put the birds away.

Cathy said, "I put my fingerprint on the mantle today."

She smiled at her husband, and took the dead birds from him, and slipped her arm through his.

Arm in arm, man and wife, we all walked back to the house.

BELOVED CRITTERS

A LITTLE SQUIRRELLY

by Nancy Knight

*You enter into a certain amount of madness when you marry a
person with pets.*
—Nora Ephron

C hildren love animals and would keep a
menagerie of pets if they could. Mama
would never let us have pets, except for Mr.
Thomas, an old tom cat that took up at our house
during the summer after I turned three. He always
stayed outside. Mr. Thomas was a great hunter, always bringing little snakes, moles, and mice up to the
house and placing them on the front porch for us to
see. Mama couldn't stand even the idea of a critter
in the house, no matter how well groomed and trained
it was—and no matter how good a hunter.

When I was in the first grade, we moved to
Cleveland Park, giving Mr. Thomas a huge hunting
ground to prowl. My sister and I were old enough by
then to discover plenty of critters in need of a home,
and we always brought them home. Like the duckling we found one time at Cleveland Park Lake. Or
the chicken we found pecking beneath a large oak in
the picnic area. There was always an assortment of

72

baby birds, bird eggs, frogs, and bugs—none of which were to Mama's liking. She sent each and every one of them back into the wild from which they came, despite our tears, pouts and protests.

Looking back, I suspect that the duckling's own mama was searching for him. And the chicken probably belonged some neighbors on the street behind ours. But at the time, of course, Mama's logic meant nothing to us.

Daddy, on the other hand, was always on our side when it came to house pets. He loved animals—all of them. He, too, would have liked a houseful of pets if he could have sweet-talked Mama into it.

He got his chance when the city cut down the beautiful old oak trees beside the service station he owned and a family of squirrels got displaced. He couldn't do much for the mother squirrel, but she could fend for herself. It was the three helpless babies that bothered him.

Daddy decided he would just have to serve as Mama to those babies. He and the men who worked for him built a huge cage of chicken wire, replete with a human's approximation of a squirrel nest, an enclosed area for privacy, and lots of sunny places with tree limbs where they could play. They even made one of those running wheels so the squirrels could get some exercise. They set the cage up in front of the service station, close to the place their tree had once been.

The babies were too young to eat solid food at first, so Daddy went down to Kress's Five and Dime and bought a few doll bottles to feed them. The local veterinarian said it was probably a hopeless cause, but Daddy refused to give up. At first he fed them

Carnation Evaporated Milk. It wasn't long before he was feeding them chopped pecans or acorns when he could find them.

That squirrel cage became somewhat of a tourist attraction in the neighborhood. People would stop in, just to see how the babies were doing. The squirrels, accustomed by now to humans, would chatter excitedly when anybody stood by their cage. Somehow, they knew they were the neighborhood celebrities.

Dr. Smith's pediatrics practice, which was located next to Daddy's service station, lured in plenty of kids to see the squirrels. Pretty soon, mothers were bribing children with a visit to see the baby squirrels if they behaved properly at the doctor's office. Sometimes it worked, sometimes it didn't, but there were always lots of children peering into the cage.

Everybody seemed concerned with the welfare of those baby squirrels except Mama. When we'd go to see Daddy at work, she never ventured near their cage. She always said they looked like rats with fuzzy tails to her. Maybe they did, but my sister Joyce and I didn't care. We loved to play with them. We may have been mistaken, but I swear those babies' big black eyes would light up when we approached.

All of the babies adored Daddy, but the runt of the litter was his favorite. Peanut was a smart little fur-ball. Daddy carried him in his coat pocket most of the time. He even taught him a few tricks. After a while, Daddy could place a pecan on the office counter and say, "Peanut, ole buddy, you want a pecan?"

That little squirrel would poke his head out of Daddy's pocket, run up his arm and around his shoulders, dash down the other arm, and grab that nut.

He'd tuck it away in Daddy's jacket pocket for a rainy day. He never seemed to figure out that it was always the same nut.

One night, Daddy forgot that Peanut was in his pocket when he came home. He hung his jacket on one of the dining room chairs as he always did. Peanut was content to sleep in Daddy's pocket, but some time during the night he got a little hungry and started munching on that pecan.

The crunch of breaking pecan shells woke Mama up. She grabbed a broom out of the broom closet and began to hunt down the "rat" which had somehow gotten into our house. Imagine her surprise when she tracked the sounds to Daddy's coat pocket. She was just about to swat the coat with the broom when Daddy stopped her. Needless to say, she was very unhappy about the squirrel in the house—especially one that made sounds like a rat.

Daddy promised never to forget and leave a squirrel in his pocket again, and, the excitement over, we all went back to bed. Well, that was a pie crust promise: easily made and easily broken.

Several weeks later, Daddy forgot to put Peanut in his cage again a day or so before Thanksgiving. He came in, took off his jacket, and hung it on the dining room chair as usual. We had supper and then went off to complete our homework. Daddy sat down to watch the news in front of our new Admiral television set. It was our second one—ever so much better than the tiny picture tube of our first.

After a while, we joined Daddy in the living room to watch television. We curled up next to him on the couch, nestled into his arms, and settled in for one of our favorite programs. We never missed *Our*

Miss Brooks if we could help it. And it was a show we liked to watch together.

All the while Peanut snoozed quietly in Daddy's pocket.

Mama was in the kitchen making a pecan pie to take to Granny's for Thanksgiving while we watched television. The rooms were arranged in a manner that allowed her to listen to the television, but not see it. Occasionally, she would pop in to see what that silly Walter Denton (played by a young Richard Crenna) was up to. All in all, it was one of those comfortable evenings when we were all together.

After a while, Peanut must have smelled the pecans Mama was shelling—his favorite treat—and began to search for a snack. Or he may have been attracted by the voices, since he was accustomed to being around people. But, for whatever reason, he was no longer satisfied to sleep in his most loved place. He climbed out of Daddy's pocket and scurried into the kitchen. Mama, suspecting nothing out of the ordinary, continued to shell pecans and talk back and forth with us about the show and the upcoming holiday.

The baby squirrel might have been confused at first. He probably saw the counter and wondered how he could get way up there for his nut. He finally figured out a way to reach the counter top, looking for that pecan Daddy always teased him with, and began his ascent. Unfortunately, the route he took was straight up Mama's leg.

Her scream jolted us into action. With Daddy leading the way, my sister and I dashed into the kitchen. Mama stood cowering in the narrow slot between the refrigerator and the kitchen table. Peanut crouched, shivering with fear, between the cabinets, with no place to hide.

Daddy, after insuring that Mama hadn't injured herself, reached down and picked Peanut up. He tried his best to comfort the frightened squirrel, but it continued to quiver with fear. Nothing seemed to help, not Daddy's calming voice, not the hands of two little girls trying to pet him and cuddle him. Eventually, Mama couldn't stand to see the little critter so scared, so she edged over to the bowl of pecans and nudged it toward Daddy. He kind of grinned that sheepish grin of his and offered one of the shelled pecans to Peanut. "Peanut, ole buddy, you want a pecan?"

That did the trick. Peanut took the pecan and nibbled on it until the shaking stopped. Daddy put him down on the counter, and he ate another piece of pecan with Mama watching warily from her vantage point beside the Frigidaire.

Mama breathlessly told us how she'd been standing there, working away. A couple of times she heard a scratching sound, but dismissed the noises as coming from the television set. And then, "That creature jumped onto my leg, caught hold of my stockings, climbed to my knee, up my skirt, and leapt to the counter."

Joyce and I shrieked with laughter at the idea of cute little Peanut climbing Mama's leg. Her shredded stockings weren't funny though. Daddy had to promise to buy her another pair.

That was Mama's up close and personal introduction to Peanut and I don't think she was too happy about it.

From then on, she always asked Daddy where the squirrels were. I think she and Peanut finally reached a truce. On the rare occasions when he'd come home with Daddy, she'd always find a few nuts to put in the pocket for our "guest" to nibble on during the night. She didn't want to take a chance on him venturing out to find food and climbing her leg again.

Back at the service station, folks just loved to watch Peanut do his trick. Every day somebody would stop by and ask Daddy to do it. He'd grin and say, "Peanut, ole buddy, you want a pecan?" Sure enough, Peanut would poke his head out of the pocket and scurry out to get his pecan.

Remember, I told you that Peanut was a smart little fur-ball? Well, one day Daddy was pulling his favorite trick and Peanut, just as always, raced around Daddy's shoulders to get his pecan. But this time, instead of putting it in Daddy's pocket, he dashed out the front door and buried it in the pansy garden that bordered the office.

Eventually, Daddy began to leave the cage open so the babies, who were now grown, could begin to see what a squirrel's world was really like. One by one, they ventured out to see the world at the corner of St. John Street and Oakland Avenue there in Spartanburg. They'd prowl about, but always come back to the cage.

Gradually they left to have families of their own. But for more than a year, three baby squirrels were the most popular attraction in the area—except to Mama.

And, I suspect that, to this day, every time she makes a pecan pie, she glances over her shoulder just to make sure Peanut isn't there behind her, planning to use her nylon clad legs like a tree trunk.

UP JUMPS THE DEVIL

by Donna Ball

I'm a lean dog, a keen dog, a wild dog, and lone.
—Irene Rutherford McLeod

In 1782 my ancestors came down out of the hills of North Carolina and shrewdly negotiated the Indians out of some fifteen hundred acres of prime North Georgia farm land. A generation later, my great-great-great-great-grandfather took a fancy to the daughter of a Cherokee chief and sought her father's permission to marry. The price of the chief's blessing: two thousand acres of prime North Georgia farm land. Since red clay acreage back in those days was one thing that even my folks—for whom the phrase dirt poor was invented—had no trouble acquiring in abundance, the dowry was easily paid with a few hundred acres left over.

There are, in fact, two things that all native Georgians worth their peanuts have in common, if you look deeply enough into the weeds that obscure the family tree: the once-upon-a-time ownership of great sprawling expanses of land, and a Cherokee princess ancestor. My illustrious forebear may well have gotten more than he bargained for in this particular deal, however: twelve children, a mission school, and a Cherokee princess who turned out to be a boot-wearing, whip-wielding tyrant who patrolled the school grounds with a shotgun under one arm, the whip in the other, and a Bowie knife tucked into the cuff of her boot—thereby eliminating some of the discipline problems that plague the public school system today.

Eventually there came, of course, the Trail of Tears, and another great land deal—although most Cherokee would not describe it in precisely that way. It worked out pretty well for my great-great, however, as he was able to recoup most of what the family had lost in the Great Dowry Exchange—and promptly deeded it over to his wife, who was, of course, Cherokee and unable to own property. Gone again.

And so it continued over the next several generations, for if there was one thing my family was better at than acquiring land, it was losing it in bad deals. A thousand acres won in a poker game. Six hundred lost to cotton speculation and boll weevils. Eight hundred gained in a wily railroad deal, twelve hundred lost when the deal fell through. By the turn of the century my family had paid for the original two thousand acres a dozen times, and had only managed to hold on to five hundred.

During the Depression my great-grandfather deeded one hundred twenty acres to his son-in-law Early Hall, only to shoot that same Mr. Hall in the back two years later when he found him *in flagrante delicto* with a woman not his wife. It was a mortal wound, but justice being what it was in those days—my great-gramps was a pillar of the community and all the Halls had to back them up was a bunch of hillbilly white trash living in mill shacks on the edge of the woods– he never even went to trial. Times were hard enough, most folks figured, without a body having to worry about who was doing what with whose wife, and besides, who was going to take care of the poor widow now if her daddy went to jail?

And that, plus or minus a few dozen acres here and there, was how the situation stood as we entered the last half of the twentieth century: the original two thousand acres parceled up to small farms all around, each one representing a misdeed, a sentimental moment, or a lapse in judgement, with my family's three hundred or so acres sitting smack dab in the middle. My grandfather, then eighty-three years old and failing, had a cynical and ultimately pragmatic view of the burdens of land ownership. Upon their marriages he had offered each of his four children a chance to buy fifty acres of their heritage; what was left over, he swore, he was going to let the government have when he died. The dad-blamed land had caused enough trouble over the years in his estimation and he would be glad to get shed of it.

His impression that the government confiscated all property that was left intestate was of course mistaken—they only took most of it—but we were assured one grand squabble over the remains when my grandfather was gone. Of the four children, only three survived. Two, my father and his older brother, had taken the practical route of buying out their own inheritances. My uncle had sold his fifty acres to the first Baptist Church and moved to California; there was now a brand-new Fellowship Hall where the watermelon patch used to be, and plans were well underway for a Youth Ministries baseball field on the bottom land. My father built himself a nice ranch house opposite the old home place and raised a family, where he lived until his death.

There remained only my Aunt Millie, who had nothing to show for herself in the way of an inheritance and who, as she approached, then passed, middle age, found that fact increasingly nettlesome. If Grandpa died without a will, the remaining two hundred acres would be divided three ways after taxes and probate fees, leaving the boys with a total of one hundred and five acres each and Aunt Millie with only fifty five. This was, as any reasonable person could see, monumentally unfair.

In 1983 Aunt Millie, who had spent the past thirty years living the high life in Atlanta and doing her best to put her humble beginnings on a North Georgia dirt farm behind her, was stricken by nostalgia—and possibly by an acute awareness of the soaring resale values of north Georgia real estate—and moved back home to nurse her ailing father through what he insisted would be his last year on earth. Of course, Grandpa had been insisting he was living his last year on earth for the past eight years, but this did not discourage Aunt Millie. By day she dedicated herself to making Grandpa's last days the most comfortable of his life, borrowing against Grandpa's life insurance to replace the one hundred and fifty year old plaster walls with laminate paneling and to install vinyl siding over the wormy chestnut exterior. By night, she pursued a determined re-education program for Grandpa on the value of leaving a written will—a will that, preferably, named only one heir: his beloved only daughter.

It was around the same time that Aunt Millie moved home that another notable event occurred in the community: the birth of a litter of half German-Shepherd/ half Lab puppies to Willard Hall—a descendant of the very same Hall who Great-Grandpa hadn't simply killed, but to whom he had referred for the rest of his life as "that low down thieving s.o.b. that stole my land and ruint my daughter." (Great-Aunt Iris, it should be said, bore her ruination well. She went on to marry a doctor in Macon, bear him six children, and die at the age of eighty-two a wealthy and contented widow who, to all appearances, never once looked back upon her tragic past).

By this time both the relationship and the feud had been mostly forgotten, although members of my family still referred to the Halls as "shiftless" and the Halls, more likely than not, would spit great brown streams of tobacco juice on the ground whenever a male member of my family passed. They were still living on the land Great-Gramps had deeded out in 1933, having parceled it up to accommodate single-wides and leans-tos for whichever members of their family needed a place to light.

What used to be lush green meadowland was now criss-crossed with bulldozed dirt driveways and chicken-scratched yards, clotheslines sagging with dingy laundry and bare-chested children standing around with their fingers in their noses. Whenever you drove up one of those dirt tracks, a big dog would chase your car—a different dog every time—and then stand splayed-legged and wild-eyed, barking a bark that rattled the car windows until you blew your horn loud enough to make someone come out of the house, haul the dog off, and tie him up.

My brother was, around this time, just getting settled in Athens in his new job and first real apartment, and he decided his life just wasn't complete without a dog. Naturally, when he heard the Halls had a litter, he concluded that was where he would go to get his new pup.

He arrived at feeding time, so he tells the story. A raw-boned black Lab bitch, a male dog that quite possibly had German Shepherd ancestry, and eight fat tail-wagging puppies were face deep in a shallow dishpan filled with kibble. Another pup, who had apparently not heard the dinner bell, came galloping up just then and belly-flopped into the middle of the dish. The German Shepherd, startled, growled at the pup. The pup growled back. The German Shepherd backed off.

For all of you out there who are considering bringing a new puppy to share your lives and your homes, the following advice will not fail you: do not choose the one who, at age eight weeks, is already so mean he scares his own daddy.

For my brother, however, no other dog would do. This was one tough little guy. This was a dog with spirit. This was a *man's* dog. Coal black, bigger than his brothers and sisters by half, faster than lightning and meaner than you-know-what, my brother named him, appropriately enough, Lucifer.

I wasn't there, but I imagine old Willard was grinning as my brother drove off with little Lucifer under his arm. On that day, it seems to me, an old score was finally settled.

Lucifer's adolescence proceeded predictably. Some dogs eat light bills; this dog ate lamps. He cut his teeth on automobile chassis and railroad ties; he was demolishing poodles at age six months. He was one of the few dogs not only to be kicked out of puppy kindergarten, but banned from all dog schools within a seventy-five-mile radius.

Those dog trainers are a spiteful lot, and they have an underground network you simply would not believe.

By the time he was a year old Lucifer was approximately the size of a truck, filled with a joyful and exuberant spirit, and possessed of a stubborn streak that was unmatched anywhere in nature. What he loved, he loved intensely, and that included almost all people, flower beds, car rides, food of any description, and runs in the park. What he hated he tended to kill on sight, and the less said about that the better.

For my brother, who was living in his first apartment with two roommates, the blessings Lucifer brought into his life were mixed, to say the least. On the one hand, there was the joy of early morning runs and being greeted in the evenings by big, wet, slobbery kisses. On the other hand, there was the fact that his roommates—not to mention his dates—were afraid to enter the apartment before being armed with a large sturdy stick. Several of them—dates and roommates—had been flattened by the exuberant puppy, and everyone who had ever visited the apartment bore at least one scar from being happily jumped upon and clawed by the canine welcoming committee.

The end came, alas, when Lucifer jumped up for a better view of the meter reader, who had the audacity to cross his visual path without permission, and shattered the six-hundred-dollar plate glass window in my brother's living room. It was generally

85

agreed upon by all concerned that Lucifer would be much happier as a country dog. He went to live with my mother.

My mother, recently widowed and in no way desirous of either the protection or the companionship Lucifer was supposed to afford her, tolerated the new addition to her homestead by setting a few simple rules: No dogs in the house. No poop on the lawn. No barking after midnight. Other than that, he was on his own. Surprisingly enough, Lucifer acceded to these minimum requirements in exchange for two squares a day and a soft rug on the porch on which to sleep. My mother and he established what might be referred to as a separate peace, while elsewhere in the neighborhood, war raged.

Who stole the rack of ribs off the Bootheby's grill right under Commissioner Bootheby's nose? All anyone ever saw was a black blur. And what about the missing guinea hens over at Rock Mableton's place? Nothing but a pile of feathers and some giant paw prints in the mud in the way of evidence. Lilly Hancock, however, caught him red-handed, tangled up in the clothesline and a brand-new J.C. Penney half slip, the remainder of her whites trampled in the mud. Lucifer just stood there, grinning at her affably, and when she came at him with a broom, he loped off, taking her half-slip with him.

But of all the neighbors with whom Lucifer had, shall we say, managed to put something less than his best paw forward, his relationship with Aunt Millie was the most strained. It was, in fact, more aptly described as a love-hate relationship: he loved her and everything associated with her to distraction; she hated him with an almost homicidal mania. Let's skip over Lucifer's early attempts to endear himself to the heart of my aunt: the gopher guts he vomited on her new silk pumps, the UPS package he found on her doorstep and thoughtfully opened for her—scattering bladder-control pads all over the front yard—the annoying yard cat he quickly disposed of out of the goodness of his heart. The real line in the sand was drawn, so to speak, over the peony bushes.

Since returning to the home place and deciding that, as soon as Grandpa changed his will, she would be able to make a very nice life for herself here, Aunt Millie had done her best to become an influential member of the community. She joined the Garden Club, the Eastern Star, and the First Baptist Church. She had made a point to endear herself to all the most important people in the community, and when she learned that one of our cousins—a very distant cousin several times removed—was actually running for the Georgia House of Representatives, she worked vigorously on his campaign simply for the hope of one day being able to toss in a casual conversational reference to "Cousin Lloyd, down at the State Capitol."

As it happened, her efforts were rewarded, and Cousin Lloyd actually won a seat. Aunt Millie was beside herself with joy. We were Uptown now. We were Somebody. We were going to give a party and let the whole county know we had friends in high places.

The gathering, a combination family reunion and old fashioned "dinner on the grounds" that Southerners so adore, was planned for the Saturday afternoon before the spring Revival meeting began at the First Baptist. The preacher and the visiting evangelist would be guests of honor, as would the illustrious Cousin Lloyd. Long tables with checkered tablecloths would be set up under the oak trees, Cousin Elmo's boy Dan would play guitar music in the background, and Grandma Josie's peonies would be in full bloom, providing the perfect backdrop for the family photographs Aunt Millie was paying a professional from Atlanta seventy-five dollars an hour to take.

Peonies are a big, showy bush flower that seem to be made for the Southern garden. Grandma Josie didn't have much time for a flower garden—she was a farmer's wife, after all—but she did grow the most spectacular peony bushes in the county. After her death, Grandpa had pretty much let them go to ruin, but to her credit, Aunt Millie had brought them back. A dozen of them lined the curve of the driveway as it circled in front of the house, scarlet and pink and ruffled white. They were, in fact, quite spectacular–until Lucifer, three days before the party, chased a squirrel across the yard, around the drive, and up the oak tree.

He didn't just dive into the flowers. He plowed through them like a Mack truck, once, twice, three times. It was so much fun that when the squirrel was out of reach, Lucifer came back and used his powerful digging talents to scatter the remnants of crushed blossoms and broken stalks across the yard. When Aunt Millie came out of the house to see what the racket was about, she found Lucifer, decorated with scarlet petals and torn leaves, lying in the middle of a crushed bush, panting from his exertions and grinning happily.

Now it should be said that my mother and Aunt Millie were never destined to be the best of friends.

Mother had been heard to mutter words like "uppity" and "gold digger" to Aunt Millie's retreating back, and my aunt often sniffed the word "in-law" when she thought my mother couldn't hear. Since Lucifer had taken up residence in the community, matters between them had only deteriorated. The peonies were the last straw.

Words were exchanged which do not bear repeating. Threats were made. Doors were slammed. It ended with my mother declaring that it would take an act of God before she ever set foot in Aunt Millie's house again, and Aunt Millie declaring that if either Mother or that misbegotten son of Satan she called a dog ever crossed the street toward her house again, she would get out the shotgun. Aunt Millie stalked off with a broken peony stalk bobbing angrily in her hand, and Mother threw a German chocolate cake after her.

The day of the party dawned bright and clear. Red-checked tables set with vases of cut roses and wild flowers were arranged underneath the oak trees. Grandpa, who had been wrestled into a white shirt and Sunday britches but drew the line at wearing his dentures, was also arranged underneath the oak tree where he complained loudly and to anyone who would listen about how much this dad-blamed tom-foolery was costing him. One by one the cars came up the drive, proceeded past the ruined peonies, and stopped at the front door, disgorging ladies in flowered silks bearing covered dishes, and gentlemen who hitched up their trousers and cast an uneasy glance around to try to catch the tone of the shindig before calling out a hail and hearty greeting to my grandfather.

Aunt Millie made exaggerated fusses and wide

protestations of "Oh, you shouldn't have!" and "It's too much, really!" over every dish that was uncovered and set proudly on an already overburdened table—despite the fact that she had been counting for weeks on each and every dish to feed her hungry horde of guests. Platters of fried chicken and country ham. Cold sliced pork roast, mounds of coleslaw, feathery yeast rolls and big shiny rounds of cornbread. Cut glass relish dishes were filled to overflowing with bright cucumber pickles and spicy chow-chow. Jello molds shimmered with their burden of suspended fruit and wept green and red puddles in the heat. Casserole after casserole was squeezed onto the table— sweet potato casserole, green bean casserole, squash casserole, company potato casserole, corn casserole, chicken and dressing casserole. Pitchers of sweet tea and lemonade punctuated every table. Three churns of ice cream were going on the back porch, hand-cranked by those unfortunate young cousins who weren't smart enough to get out of the way when Aunt Millie was looking for volunteers. An entire table bearing nothing but cakes and pies was set up inside.

The guests of honor, as was only proper, were among the last to arrive. First came the preacher and his wife, bearing the visiting evangelist and the preacher's wife's Sunday Ambrosia in the back seat of their silver El Dorado. Barely had Aunt Millie managed to gush a protest over how the preacher's wife shouldn't have brought anything and smile a flustered greeting to the evangelist in the back seat when the Cadillac bearing Cousin Lloyd, his wife, and his eighty-six-year-old mother pulled up behind the El Dorado. Aunt Millie was torn. Could she rush off to greet her celebrity guest while leaving the evangelist behind?

What disastrous timing. Why hadn't she planned the arrival of the cars better?

And while Aunt Millie stood there, agonizing, someone whose timing was always impeccable took the decision out of her hands.

The look on Aunt Millie's face as she turned to see Lucifer, tail high and grinning widely, round the drive and lope toward the picnic tables should be forever frozen in time. John the Revealer might have had much the same look on his face as he witnessed the arrival of the Four Horsemen of the Apocalypse.

Amid much shrieking and drawing back of silk skirts from muddy paws, Lucifer made his boisterous way through the crowd and toward the smell of food. Aunt Millie, who knew a genuine disaster when she saw one, screamed, "Lucifer!" at the top of her lungs.

Delighted to have been called by the one woman whose attention he sought more than any other's in the world, Lucifer altered his course ninety degrees and made a bee-line toward Aunt Millie. Cousin Lloyd was bending down to take from his mother's hands her prize-winning chess pie as she got out of the car when Lucifer burst between them. The pie went flying. So did the elderly woman, right back into the front seat of the Caddy, flat on her back with her skirt up over her head. Cousin Lloyd lurched backwards, slipped on the pie, and landed on his sit-upon in the dirt.

The visiting evangelist was coming out of the back seat with the Sunday Ambrosia in his hands, grinning a broad evangelical grin that indicated he had yet to become aware of the chaos that was taking place outside the car, when Lucifer, distracted by his second most favorite thing in the world—an open car door—made a detour. He jumped in the back seat and landed with both front paws flat in the middle of the Sunday Ambrosia, turned and slapped the evangelist in the face with his tail, then heard Aunt Millie screaming his name again and leapt out of the car, upsetting the rest of the ambrosia in the evangelist's lap.

He paused only to scoop up a bite or two of chess pie from the ground next to the dazed-looking State Representative, then obeyed Aunt Millie's call—with two paws on her shoulders and a big wet kiss across her Revlon-rouged face. She screamed. Grandpa cackled with laughter and waved his cane in the air. The young boys abandoned their ice cream churns and came to cheer Lucifer on. Some enterprising young matron tried to shoo Lucifer away with an embroidered napkin, which he gleefully snatched from her hand and shook until it was dead.

Second Cousin Sue Ella came out of the house just then, screeched when she saw the huge black dog mauling the napkin, and ran back into the house, slamming the screen door behind her. Lucifer took this as an invitation to join the fun inside, and bounded up the steps and through the screen door, never once noticing that the door was closed. Pies and cakes flew as he skidded onto the table. Aunt Millie covered her face with her hands and wailed as Lucifer bounded back out the door again, his muzzle white with cream pie filling.

By that time the crowd was getting mean. Someone found a broom. Someone else a two-by-four. Grandpa was laughing so hard tears ran down his weathered cheeks, and loudly declaring this the best damn party he'd been to since VE-Day. A great many of the guests joined him in loud, screeching, doubled-over shouts of laughter, but those who weren't laughing were chasing Lucifer. After once or twice around the picnic tables, Lucifer apparently decided that the fun had gone out of this adventure. The last anyone saw of him he was bounding over the peony bushes, a Tupperware bowl of Chinese chicken salad clutched in his jaws.

Lucifer did not come home that day, or that night, or the next day. Unkind speculations were made about the chicken salad, and Mother, though she had never shown much in the way of affection for the big brute before, was visibly worried. My brother came home from Athens to comb the woods for his errant friend, but to no avail. Lucifer was gone.

It was a grim group that filled the family pew on Sunday night to open the Revival meeting. Aunt Millie, pale and stiff and fortified, it was rumored, by something a little stronger than sweet tea, sat on the aisle and stared straight ahead without blinking during the entire two and three-quarter hour service. Grandpa snored beside her, interrupting his somnolence now and then to chortle out loud. Mother, on the opposite aisle, sniffed delicately into a handkerchief, although if asked to testify none of us could honestly declare whether it was tears or giggles that she was hiding. On the front row State Representative Lloyd Calhoun, sporting the latest fashion in neck braces, loudly Amened every mention the evangelist made of the consequences awaiting the followers of the devil.

The evangelist preached fire and brimstone with a particular vengeance, said those in attendance, with eyes that blazed and fists that thumped and a memory, perhaps, of Sunday Ambrosia all over his new dress pants. Sinners trembled, and even the righteous sank low in their pews. The power of the Lord was so great upon that place, praise Jesus, that midway through the sermon a great clap of thunder blew out the lights, and the heavens opened to pour down torrents of rain. After twenty minutes or so without air-conditioning the sanctuary became too stuffy for even the righteous to bear, and a thoughtful deacon opened up the outer doors to admit the cooling breeze and the smell of cleansing rain. The choir took its place as the invitational began. Filled with the Spirit, the evangelist tore off his tie, rolled up his sleeves, stretched out his arms, and sweated and wept openly as he begged the unrepentant to come to Jesus before it was too late.

The choir had reached the third verse of "Just As I Am" and no one had moved. Tensions were running high. Mother shot dark looks at Aunt Millie, and Aunt Millie remained stoic. Grandpa snored. The evangelist left the pulpit and stood before the altar, arms outstretched, face turned heavenward as he prayed, beseeched, entreated an Almighty God to strike repentance into the black souls of the sinners cowering in their pews.

And then something happened. Murmurs of astonishment and whispers of awe undulated from back to front through the audience. Heads turned, necks craned, gasps were subdued. And who should come strolling up the aisle, wet to the skin and seeking absolution—or perhaps seeking nothing more than shelter from the rain—but Lucifer himself. Head high, tail wagging, he walked straight into the evangelist's open arms—thus giving that man of God the singular distinction of having saved the soul of the devil himself.

Oh, and Aunt Millie? She did, in fact, get what she wanted. Joe Bob Ramey, the family lawyer, said that Grandpa made his will that very Monday after the party, and it was his opinion that the old man was persuaded to do so out of nothing more than pure appreciation for the show his daughter had put on with that dog. Nine months and six days later, Aunt Millie was the proud owner of two hundred acres of prime North Georgia real estate, which she promptly put on the market at five thousand dollars an acre.

The first offer she got was for a mere seventy five acres, from a developer who was known for his upscale golf and tennis communities. Exercising the shrewd negotiating skills for which my family is renowned, Aunt Millie offered him his pick of the acreage—at six thousand an acre. Hardly daring to believe his luck, the developer took her up on it, cut a check, and lost no time in registering the deed to his new property—which consisted of every bit of road frontage my aunt possessed.

Ten months later he bought out the remaining property, which was virtually useless without road frontage, for one hundred dollars per.

Aunt Millie, having held up the family tradition for excellent land deals, moved to Florida and is living today on Social Security.

Lucifer lived to be thirteen years old, and was buried at last on the hill east of my mother's house, overlooking the erstwhile peony bushes. My brother commissioned a granite marker for the grave.

Here lies Lucifer, it reads.

A man's dog.

COOKIE THE ONE-EYED HORSE

by Virginia Ellis

Lady Godiva put everything she had on a horse.
—W.C. Fields

When I was seven, I had three best friends: Mary Jo Taylor, a boy named Jesse, and Cookie, a one-eyed horse.

Cookie, a little more than two years old and not a plug, was of no use to my friend's father, a horse dealer, because of her obvious disability. So, Mr. Taylor had given her to Mary Jo.

We'd been told Cookie lost her eye when some mean boy had shot her with a BB gun. She looked perfectly normal except for the smooth flat place where her right eyeball used to be. Mary Jo and I didn't care that she wasn't perfect, we had a horse for a friend and since she loved cookies, that's what my friend named her.

I don't believe Cookie knew she was a horse, however. I think, perhaps because she'd suffered a trauma in her youth, she got confused. Cookie thought she was a dog. If we didn't tie her up, she'd follow us wherever we went: in the paddock, all over the yard, even up the steps to the house once, before

Mary Jo's mother opened the screen door and chased her off. She knew we were inside eating cheese sandwiches for lunch and thought she must surely be invited.

Cookie had an overall kind disposition, didn't bite or kick. She'd let us ride her double and barebacked, running like the wind through the pasture till one of us fell off. The only time she ever hurt me was when I was unlucky enough to fall underneath her at a full canter. Her back foot yanked out a whole handful of my hair and put a good sized knot on my head. It was the only time in my life I saw little circling stars like the cartoon characters when I came to.

Mary Jo and I didn't tell anybody about my spill because we didn't want them to take Cookie away from us. Later in life, when I had to have a CAT scan for a physical, I found out that Cookie's memory still resides in my grown-up self. One side of my skull is thicker—exactly where she stepped on my head.

Now I guess that means I can claim I wasn't always so hard-headed. I don't bother to do so, however, because I doubt anyone who knows me would buy it.

When you live out in the farm country of Florida, you don't have a wide choice of kids to play with. You're fairly restricted to family and close neighbors, which is why a variety of animals became our friends and in some ways, our guardians. When you're on a horse in the same pasture with a Brahma bull the size of a Volkswagon on stilts, for example, and your horse suddenly tenses up and heads for the barn like its tail is on fire, your job is to hold on with all your fingers and toes because the horse is trying to save your life...either that or it heard sweet feed being poured from a coffee can into the trough.

But, as I mentioned, I didn't have many human playmates. Mary Jo lived on the next farm, and Jesse lived even further away. His family and most of the rest of the world existed on the other side of a canal too wide for me to imagine crossing on my own. It was a great occasion when Jesse's mother brought him over for a visit.

The three of us, Jesse, Mary Jo and I used to disappear regularly into the secret places that only kids know. Rabbit trails in the high weeds, the tangled roots of the big Australian pines lining the canal across the road, the old barn with half a roof near the big grapefruit tree in the back. That was our playground.

On one particular visit, Mary Jo and I took Jesse to meet Cookie. Although very impressed, he said he didn't think he would enjoy riding anything that big, and no, he didn't want to feed the horse a vanilla wafer. Since he was my friend I didn't want to call him a chicken, so we said goodbye to Cookie before any abject bravery was required on his part, and we walked back over to my house to see what critters we could find in the old deserted barn. I was a little concerned that Jesse might run back to his momma if we came across a snake but decided it couldn't be helped. We'd just stay away from the old tin and wood pile and hope for the best.

Jesse took one look at the barn and said, "I'm not climbing up there."

Mary Jo and I looked at each other with the same expression we might have years later if a guest sat down to our carefully prepared Thanksgiving dinner and announced, "I don't eat dead bird."

"What do you want to do then?" we asked,

almost simultaneously.

He just shrugged.

Suddenly we had nothing to do—a very unusual state of affairs for us. I moved over to the bales of hay that were stacked against the dry side of the barn and sat down. Soon Mary Jo and Jesse followed, except they had to move a bale over to make another place to sit. So we sat. And we sat.

Then, with the sudden inspiration of country kids, someone said, "Let's build a fort," and we were off. Soon we had dragged out the center bales of the square stack and built a room inside. We had to climb in over the top but once inside, the five foot outer walls completely hid us.

After all that work we had to sit down and rest awhile in our nest. It was so quiet and cool down there in the shade that we discussed having a picnic. None of us wanted to go back to the house, however, since that might mean it would be time to leave if Jesse's mother happened to be ready to go. If they couldn't find us, they couldn't make us come back.

It only took us around fifteen minutes of resting and discussing to decide to play doctor.

Now, I'm not blaming or accusing anyone—nor do I expect to get off the hook. I'll just say that at the ripe old age of seven, having lived with only sisters, I was interested to see how the other half lived, so to speak. Mary Jo had a little brother, but he was just a baby—no use to us as a playmate or a co-conspirator.

It took several choruses of, "You go first. No, you go first," to make us decide to all drop our shorts at once. So, with sweaty hands and guilty consciences from what we were about to do, we dropped trou.

This turned out to be something Jesse was very

interested in. As we gawked at each other's private parts, he seemed to be prouder of his than he should have been. He was just informing us how we were slighted because we didn't get a pee-pee when the walls started to shake.

You must have heard the expression, Putting the Fear of God into someone. Well, we were so panic-stricken we were competition for Lot's wife. I looked toward the blue sky thinking we'd been caught by my grandmother's hell-and-damnation God, or worse, by my grandmother herself who would stripe my backside until even the thought of baring it would be painful, and I was too transfixed to pull up my panties.

The walls moved again, even more violently. As if we'd been ordered, all three of us yanked up our pants and turned to face our doom.

That's when Cookie looked over the top of our fort, and if a horse could smile, she was grinning from ear to ear.

I have to say that I had the urge to smile as well—mostly from nervous relief at not being required, this time, to pay the price for my curiosity about boys. But the relief I felt about not facing symbolic death at the hands of our parents was overshadowed, just like we were overshadowed by Cookie. I realized that that silly dog/horse had climbed up the pile of hay bales, and the way they were shaking meant they were about to come down as suddenly as the house of straw so carefully constructed by the Three Little Pigs.

It would do no good to order Cookie to get down. If anything, she would most likely try to jump in the center with us.

"Climb out! Climb out!" this little piggy yelled as I headed for a side of bales that wasn't teetering under Cookie's full grown horse weight. We scampered out of there like hysterical mice and then stood on the ground admiring Cookie's tenacity. Even without an eye she'd followed us and found us without regard to her safety. Ours either.

It took some thinking to get Cookie down from her perch. It's a heck of a lot easier to get a horse to go forward than it is to shift them in reverse, especially a horse who only has a single-eyed view of the world. But Cookie trusted us. Both Mary Jo and I got back up on the bales to show Cookie the way down. By the time we'd done that, Jesse said he thought he wanted to go home.

Jesse never came back to visit me, but I didn't miss him much. Cookie was around for many more years and proved a better friend. I can still remember her playful nudges and the smell of her warm horse breath, spiced by vanilla wafers.

I hope wherever she is now, and I assume that to be horse heaven, she can see as far as the horizon. And I'd like to think she remembers two young girls who loved her.

FAMILY PORTRAITS

FROM WHENCE WE COME

by Debra Dixon

The past is never where you think you left it.
—-Katherine Anne Porter

Southerners are pedigreed. We're catalogued and classified like anthropological treasures in Bubba Tut's tomb. And we've no one to blame but ourselves. Something about being Southern creates an emptiness inside the soul that can only be filled by "our people."

While any genealogist worth her salt can slap together a passable family tree, words on paper aren't enough to impress us. We don't care who your great-great-great-great grandfather was or how many times he met the queen. What we want to know is whether or not you have the coat he was married in. Or the first pair of shoes he bought for his children. Or the three teacups and five saucers your great Aunt Precious didn't break over Uncle Dickie's head when he came home too drunk to know he smelled like adultery.

Our love affair with the past begins early. My sister and I never needed Aesop's fables or the Brothers Grimm. In the South, if you need a bedtime story—pick a relative. Need inspiration? Pick a relative. Need a moral? Pick a relative. (Don't throw china when you're angry. Don't drink and drive women wild.)

Every tiny detail of our physical being and personality can be traced to Aunt Box's fascination with door-to-door salesmen or Nana Burk's thick ankles. Keeping these people, their memories, vividly alive in our souls comes naturally to Southerners. Every family has a storyteller—the keeper of our identity, the collector of our frailties. My sister is ours, despite the fact that she possesses an oddly selective memory.

Her fines at the library are so high that it's usually cheaper to pretend the books are lost and buy them. But she can remember every secret the family has or ever hinted at having. She's managed to scrounge an impressive collection of old family photographs that originally belonged to gullible kinfolk who didn't realize the innocent-sounding question, "May I borrow this?" was actually code for "You may never see this again."

No irate cousin has yet taken her to court over custody of the photo album, but we live in fear the day will come. (Faded sepia photographs are a status symbol of the South.) Mama will rush to the courthouse, arriving early as always and prepared to defend her child to the death. Sis won't be there. The summons will have been lost in the bowels of her beat-up Ford filing cabinet—important papers in the front seat, junk mail in the back.

She's got her own compass for navigating life, and it generally gets her where she wants to go. But then she's fond of scenic routes and dead ends. With her it's always the journey, not the destination, that's important.

Our parents' first clue that their two girls were dramatically different should have been the home movies of Christmas. My sister would pull something from her stocking and dance around the room, completely absorbed by the joy of the moment. (Mama would finally tell her that tissue paper wasn't a toy, and Sis would dive back into the stocking for another discovery.) The contents of my stocking were lined up neatly along the couch cushion.

When we dressed our new Barbies for the fashion parade, my poor Barbie was dressed in a sensible brown business suit. Her Barbie tripped the light fantastic in a sparkling magenta party dress just dripping with spangles.

Now that you know Sis a bit better, you can appreciate our skepticism when she decided to find the past—Daddy's past. The whole unsettling issue of Daddy and his people had been worrying her for twenty years, right from the moment she'd discovered he was adopted—half-adopted actually.

We'd lived in blissful ignorance of Daddy's past until our teenage years—until the government declined to issue Sis her Social Security card. Apparently there existed a teensy discrepancy with the names on a birth certificate. Daddy very calmly explained that the man we'd thought of as our grandfather, the man who died when we were quite young, wasn't a blood relative. No, he wasn't interested in finding his biological father. No, he wasn't interested in discussing details. Case closed.

And that, Daddy expected, was the end of that.

For a smart man, a homicide detective—a man known to analyze minute bits of information and apprehend dumbfounded criminals, he made one major miscalculation. He thought he was dealing with business-suit Barbie. Nope. Party-dress Barbie was on the case. Somewhere, there existed another grandfather. Maybe uncles and aunts and cousins. Oh, my!

He'd just handed the family storyteller a blank page—a blank page that nagged her and reminded her for twenty years that she wasn't doing her job. Every couple of years she'd ask another question. Get another answer. Quietly, she began compiling a meager cache of information.

By the time she confessed to Daddy that she had a need to find his people (and steal their photographs), she knew these things:

- Daddy's people came from East Tennessee.
- Daddy's daddy had a name—Byrd Daugherty.
- Byrd had been a coal miner who'd lost part of an index finger in a mine accident.
- The family had lived in Chicago for a time.
- When Daddy was two, his mother left his father and moved back to the South.
- Daddy had never been contacted by his father, not at Christmas, not on birthdays.

I've got to tell you...the lack of solid leads was enough to daunt business-suit Barbie. For party-dress Barbie it seemed an impossible task.

Sis had looked for any number of things during her thirtysomething years and never found any of them. Well, technically...she never finished looking for them. Living in the "moment," as Sis does, is fraught with distractions. Entire game plans had been abandoned by her in the blink of an eye for butterflies, garage sales, and men who were completely wrong for the family. (In the South, it must be understood, you don't marry the woman, you marry the family.)

Given her track record, we never expected this newest quest to amount to much, but—being Southern—we understood her need to try.

Weeks turned into months turned into years. She charmed complete strangers into tearing out or copying sections of their telephone directories so she could send letters in and around Chicago to anyone possessing the same last name as our grandfather. Or anything sounding remotely similar to Daugherty. Genealogy experts gave her pointers and even shared some of their research. The Internet as we know it didn't exist in the early Nineties. The television program *Unsolved Mysteries* wasn't on the tube.

Each tiny breakthrough seemed to lead to another dead end. Most anyone else would have given this up as a lost cause, but Sis's quirky compass was finally coming in handy. She'd been in training for dead ends all her life. Somewhere out there were uncles and aunts and cousins. And she was determined to find them.

One night an amateur genealogist called and said she'd found our people. We learned that Daugherty is a fairly common name in the East Tennessee mountains, but if you go back far enough they're all related. (You have to go back to the 1860's. Two Daugherty brothers couldn't agree on whether to wear blue or grey during the "great unpleasantness with the North." Tempers flared. As a result the clan split, and to this day each brother's descendants live on different sides of the mountain and don't speak. Apparently, pigheadedness is hereditary.)

After a pregnant pause, our helpful genealogist strongly suggested we not try and visit "our people" since they tend to answer their doors armed with automatic weapons and intensely distrust strangers. On one occasion she'd been fired upon and promptly lost interest in that branch of her family tree, thus ending her research.

What she had amassed, she offered to forward and Sis gladly accepted. The care package included more warnings about bullets, research notes, family trees, names, directions to Daugherty cemeteries, and what is now known in family lore as The Map. (Any map with a building marked "the snake handling church" deserves legendary status.) Despite the dire warnings—accompanied by the unwelcome news that the man we were looking for had died—Sis planned a trip. There was a cemetery to visit. A headstone to touch. A widow to talk with.

Sis needed closure to the longest journey of her life. She needed to put a face to those people. Our storyteller had a need to touch history.

Mama, ever protective of her children, didn't mind her touching history, but she didn't want her touching snakes and catching bullets. Two bodyguards were assigned—Mama's brother, who has a Masters in Forestry from the University of Tennessee-Knoxville, and our step-father, who was an Eagle Scout. I figured if Sis got lost in the wilderness, needed to build a lean-to and identify edible bark...she was all set. I was less clear on how these gentlemen were going to stop buckshot or any other projectile.

My money was on Sis' best-friend, who tagged along for the ride. She had three kids. I figured she could handle a few liquored-up rowdies with nothing more than "the look."

Their first stop was a mountain cemetery carved out of wilderness. Our grandfather's sharply cut granite headstone seemed out of place with the chipped and worn stones of graves two hundred years old. He'd only died a few years earlier. That stung. Sis had found him but would never have the answers to her questions.

Did he have the same huge hands that Daddy had?

Did he love the water and dams the way Daddy did?

Did he read those stupid encyclopedias just for fun?

Could he see the fib in your eyes before the lie left your lips—the way Daddy could?

And a million more.

No stranger to deadends, Sis simply re-routed. She found a phone booth and called the number included with her notes. The phone was answered by a middle-aged masculine voice. There were sounds of a family dinner in the background. Giggles and voices and clattering dishes.

Perfect timing. If you're going to drop a bomb, Sunday Dinner is the preference of most Southerners. So, Sis dove right into her spiel. "Excuse me, you don't know me but I may be your father's granddaughter."

The conversation was quick and bizarre. Yes, his mother was the Daugherty widow in question. Absolutely no to the question of his father having been married before.

"Are you sure? Parents don't always tell us everything."

"Look...I said, no...no." But his voice wavered uncertainly.

"Okay, okay just one more question. My grandfather was missing part of an index finger from a mine acci—"

"No! Not him!" You'd have thought the man won the lottery from his enthusiasm. "Dad had all his fingers! It's not him."

Praise the Lord and pass the potatoes. Only in the South could the phrase "he had all his fingers" be a son's proud summation of his father's life.

Sis had a ten-fingered corpse and another deadend. She also had an uncle with a pocketful of quarters and an area phone book still tethered to the phone booth. No one actually expected to find our Byrd on the other end of the phone. Except maybe...Sis.

This time an older woman answered. Wouldn't call the Byrd of the household to the phone. Said it was too difficult for him to hear on the telephone even with hearing aids. She'd been married to the man for forty years and if Sis had some questions she'd better ask them of her or stop wasting her time.

Yes, he'd been married before.

Yes, he'd lived in Chicago.

And, yes, he was missing part of a finger.

"Then I'm his granddaughter."

"Well then, he'll want to talk to you. Byrd! Byrd, get the phone and hurry up. It's your granddaughter."

It was The Moment.

We've all heard about it. We talk about it. But very few of us are there to see it—the moment a grown man is brought to his knees. That's the only way Sis has ever been able to describe the first time she talked to Granddad. The first time she hugged him.

His hands are huge. As big as Daddy's. The first thing he did was put her in the car and drive her down to see the dam. He sold encyclopedias as a younger man and even read them for entertainment. Genetics are a scary thing.

But not to Southerners. We live and breathe genetics. We are who we were and are damned proud of it. We need to know that what came before will go on.

Imagine losing something very precious. Imagine your wife disappearing and taking the only child you'll ever have. Finally, when you're seventy, you stop kidding yourself. You stop looking. You put away the birth certificate and the letters and the file folders.

Then one ordinary day, when you're eighty-three, a granddaughter you've never met knocks on your door.

Imagine what it's like to want to spend one Christmas with your son before you die.

Imagine how proud I am of my sister, my family's keeper.

BIGDADDY'S OUTHOUSE

by Sandra Chastain

Man has his will—but woman has her way.
—Oliver Wendell Holmes, Sr.

M y grandparents, with whom I lived for most of my life, never nagged—at least not each other. They found other, more subtle means of making their feelings known. My grandmother was a hard-working saint. My grandfather—who I always called Bigdaddy—was close behind, at least in the sainthood department. Hardworking was another thing. To be fair, he recognized his deficiencies and took on a part time job in order to hire Slim, the local handyman, to do the chores "he didn't have time to do."

Unfortunately, Slim didn't do plumbing. Therefore, indoor plumbing didn't come to our house until I was in junior high. That never bothered my granddaddy. He'd used an outhouse all his life and continued to do so, even after the facility took a dangerous tilt to the left. Though the little weathered building was hidden from view of the neighbors by a stand of prickly plums and wormy peach trees, my grandmother wanted it gone from her chicken yard

before the next gathering of the Woman's Missionary Society, which was scheduled to meet for the first
time in years at our house. She had her egg money
and three months to accomplish her goal, both of
which might have been enough if she hadn't committed the unpardonable sin of ordering the supplies from
Mr. Weed down at the hardware store without my
granddaddy's knowledge. Once that toilet and lava-
tory were delivered, my granddaddy went into slow
motion about removing the outhouse.

My grandmother dealt with his brand of passive resistance in her own unique way. She never said
a word, but every day when she went to the chicken
yard to feed the chickens, she "rested" her back against
the leaning side of the outhouse. Later in the day,
while hoeing her little garden, she'd transfer a shovel
of "good rich dirt" from the other side of the tilting
building to the area where she intended to plant new
strawberries. The little building with the half-moon
on the door tilted more and more precariously until
finally it became apparent that, unless Granddaddy
was willing to face the southern exposure in a way he
wouldn't want to, the outhouse had to be replaced.

Thus, Slim was commissioned to demolish the
old outhouse, build and deliver a new one. "To be
painted white, like the house," Bigdaddy told my
grandmother proudly, as if that would make everything all right.

It wouldn't. My grandmother's humiliation
would be complete.

"If any of the ladies don't 'go' before they leave
home," said Bigdaddy, "they'll have a new facility,
much better than the one those missionaries have that
you women are supporting in China."

My grandmother didn't argue. She just started thinking.

Now Slim was amenable to most anything Bigdaddy asked him to do, but he considered out-houses to be beneath his dignity and conveniently ignored Bigdaddy's request. I've decided that Slim and Bigdaddy had a similar relationship to the one existing between my grandparents—selective hearing.

After several reminders from my grandmother, Bigdaddy encountered Slim downtown with his wife and children and announced that it was time Slim got on with tearing down the old and delivering the new. "And if you don't want to get your feet nasty," he added, having no truck with putting on airs, "bring those younguns of yours to help."

Now Slim might eventually have gotten around to doing the job, but having it suggested that he bring his children to help with the dirty work was the only incentive he needed to get the job over with. Bigdaddy should have taken note of the gleam in Slim's eyes as he agreed.

And so it was that a week later, about the time my grandmother's Missionary Society members gath-ered for their monthly meeting, Slim arrived and went to work dismantling the outhouse, loudly delivering it to the woodpile, plank by plank—except for the door which he leaned against the broken lumber in such a way that the blooms of the peachtree showed through the cut out of the quarter moon.

Ignoring the din of demolition, the president of the Missionary Society, Eleanor Deriso, opened the meeting with a prayer. The minutes of the last meet-ing were read and the treasurer's report given. The members bemoaned the meager amount they'd collected for their Chinese World Missions Fund and decided to have a bake sale for which my grandmother promised to contribute several of her famous strawberry pies. Finally, after a vote was taken to send Miss Sophie (who was laid up with her back) a get-well card, the clatter of demolition from the outside slowed to a stop, and the program began.

Afterward, as the ladies gathered on the screened-in side porch for strawberries and whipped cream on pound cake, Slim came driving up with the new outhouse, shining white to match the house, and complete once more with the cut-out of a quarter moon on the door. But the most remarkable thing about the new facility was the bay window on the side.

"Why, Livy," one member exclaimed, "I didn't know you were building a new..." her voice faltered for a moment before she was struck with inspiration and finished, "new tool shed."

"Neither did Lee," Grandmother said sweetly. "And it's a hot house, not a tool shed. At least it's going to be."

"Of course," another member added. "The bay window is such a nice touch. That gave it away immediately."

My grandmother gave a serene smile and nodded. "Slim is such a craftsman. He only needed a picture to understand what I wanted. I found one in Lee's Farm Journal. Lee's going to be...surprised, at what a nice job he did."

To give them credit, not one of the ladies mentioned the quarter moon cutout in the door, a sure give away that the structure had started out to be an outhouse. But they had to have suspected that their quiet, demure Olivia was up to something. Not one verbalized the fact that my granddaddy had probably commissioned Slim to build and install the last outhouse ever to be constructed within the city limits of Wadley, Georgia...and certainly the first with a bay window.

My grandmother never mentioned it either.

As usual, Slim had done his own unique job on the construction of the facility—and in the process, exercised his own brand of passive aggression. It wasn't his fault that the board he selected for the seat was full of splinters and soaked with a sweet and sticky fluid that smelled suspiciously like sorghum syrup. Slim always did the job; he just had his own way of settling his debts.

A few days later, Bigdaddy came back from town with a can of hornet spray and a window screen. "Can't believe that fool thought I needed a window," he grumbled, then gathered up his hammer and nails and retired to his new facility where he installed the first window screen in an outhouse in the county. The new screen in no way contained the puff of insecticide, nor the bees escaping what they had thought was an easier source of honey than the peach blossoms. Grandmother just smiled and said that "sometimes a man has to take his lumps before he sees the light."

Some good things came out of the venture, however. Slim installed the plumbing in the house and finally, without mentioning the change of venue, Bigdaddy took the door off his outhouse, installed a new 'shelf' and moved the little building out of the chicken yard. My Grandmother promptly turned the area where the outhouse once had rested into a strawberry patch. The peaches and plums drew honeybees like never before. The crop of fruit for the next few years was spectacular.

Grandmother never told the ladies why her hot house started out with a quarter moon on the door or how she grew such magnificent fruit. In fact, the proceeds from the sale of Livy's fruit pies made our little church the shining star in the World Missions program. My grandmother waged her own private campaign to feed the poor, starving children in China.

Because of Bigdaddy's outhouse, we never had to "clean" our plates and we got our indoor plumbing, too.

FLYING ON FRIED WINGS

by Deborah Smith

Southerners are, of course, a mythological people...Lost by choice in dreaming of high days gone and big houses burned, now we cannot even wish to escape.
—Jonathan Daniels

Southerners of all backgrounds share a love for sports, at least for certain sports, such as football and baseball, both of which will allow a person of any social persuasion the opportunity to drink beer and holler outdoors. Basketball, however, is primarily a big-city attraction, meant to be played indoors without picnics spread on the grass or giant moths swarming under the stadium lights. Plus there is very little spitting in basketball, either by the fans or players.

This alone is enough to make basketball suspicious to rural southerners, who value the freedom to expectorate in public. Nor do rural folk care much for golf or tennis. The former is an expensive waste of good hunting territory, and the latter requires that even manly men wear snug white shorts. A good ol' boy could get himself laughed at that way.

On the other hand, big-city southerners find it

hard to appreciate traditionally rural sports, such as stock-car racing, bass tournaments, and professional wrestling, all of which require a certain suspension of self-centered dignity to understand or trust. Any sport that involves oil, bait, or bodybuilders wearing sequined capes is a little too intimate for sophisticated city folk, who don't even want to know the names of their next-door neighbors.

Fans of stock-car racing have an unwritten dress code. Men wear jeans, tractor caps, big belt buckles, and some piece of clothing that advertises either Jack Daniels, Johnny Cash, or auto parts. Women wear jeans and tank tops with ads matching their menfolks'. The stock-car-mama effect is only complete if the gals keep their hair long, perm it into tight waves, and top it with poofed-up bangs that won't move in a stiff wind. Big-city southern women cannot even imagine poofed-up bangs. They have stylists named Raoul and Bruce who would faint at the very thought.

Bass tournaments are bewildering, at best. For citified sports lovers, and also, in fact, for the majority of southerners—who only care that the catfish filets are fully fried before the ice cream is finished churning—bass tournaments are interesting solely for the cheap thrills of watching big-bellied men wobble around in precarious little boats. In fact, watching men fish isn't a sport—there's nothing to watch. For all but true fishing fans, bass tournaments are as exciting as waiting for glue to harden.

Pro wrestling is not about serious competition between serious athletes. Any longtime fan knows that the whole thing's scripted, but a real southern fan doesn't care, because wrestling is, after all, male soap opera. Women have Susan Lucci; men have Hulk

Hogan. The thrill is in the sheer histrionics of the action: the drama, the plot twists, the heroes and villains, the damsels in distress, the evil seductresses, and the noble sidekicks. Add body slams and striped tights to *Days of Our Lives*, and wrestling fans would feel right at home.

Despite all the diversity of southern sports life, however, there are a few sports that haven't caught on with either the uptown or the downhome folks. Soccer is one, no matter what the cable sports channel brags about its popularity or how many polls claim that "soccer moms" are running the country. Not in the South, they're not. Grown men kicking a ball around the ground while wearing baggy shorts is just too Socialist for southerners' tastes: we need our sports to be outright dirty and dangerous, completely silly, or supremely white-glove genteel. Soccer just doesn't fit the bill in any category.

Hockey has potential because players get to beat each other up and grin without their front teeth, but you're never going to build a groundswell of support for a sport no sunbaked southern child can grow up playing—unless hell freezes over and the local Dairy Queen sets up community rinks in its walk-in freezer.

And then there is the steeplechase. It's not really a sport, it's a social event that includes horses, and except for ritzy patches of Dixiedom where pseudo-southern-royalty gallop their hunter-jumpers across the countryside in pursuit of foxes, most of us give a slow, collective, Say what? when anyone asks if we'd like to watch it. There is something vaguely embarrassing about watching little jockeys race expensive thoroughbreds around a grassy course while leaping a few fake logs. The feeling is akin to averting one's eyes when a chubby old uncle breaks into a clogging routine during a barbecue picnic.

Even so, every spring the well-to-do and/or culturally snooty trek to huge pastures outside the southern cities to attend a steeplechase. It's like the opera. You have to say you've been to one, at least once.

Entertaining corporate visitors was part of my job as a regional manager for a chain of garden nurseries, so I had been to the steeplechase several times before the year I took my Uncle Hoyt and Aunt Wesma. I knew what to expect, and they didn't, but they insisted on doing things their way. They had been doing things their way for as long as anyone in my family could remember. The universe usually adjusted to suit them.

Uncle Hoyt was big, raw-boned, grinning, green-eyed, and full of mischief, a mountain man born-and-raised, like all my uncles. And like them, he had finished high school then refused even one more minute of higher education, opting instead for an independent life of more than a dozen self-employed occupations. Several of those jobs had made him rich, the best one being a heavy equipment sales-and-leasing company he started with my Uncle Benton, who lost an arm in a bobcat accident (the machine, not the animal) and swore he'd recoup his flesh in money.

So Uncle Hoyt had several million dollars parked squarely in savings and investment accounts, though he'd never let you know it. His little joke was letting strangers think he was just another graying, fattening ol' mountain feller. In fact neither he nor Aunt Wesma stood much on ceremony, though if you carefully studied the pea-sized diamond rings she wore on her tanned and callused hands you knew you weren't looking at cubic zirconia.

She and Uncle Hoyt shopped for most of their clothes at their local discount store, and had furnished their seven-thousand-square-foot mountain log home with plain family heirlooms and a hodgepodge of rustic cedar pieces made by my Uncle JoMo (Joseph Moses,) who owned a furniture-crafting business. Oddly enough, their plain-logic code of living easily encompassed sending my cousin Mima, their only daughter, to gourmet cooking school at a luxury resort in Thailand. The trip was her graduation present when she finished law school.

"She wanted to learn how them Thais cook," Aunt Wesma explained while hosting a family pot-luck dinner of eighty or ninety relatives, "so me and her Daddy said if she was gonna hunt turkey, she oughta go straight to the turkey's gobble."

Uncle Hoyt and Aunt Wesma did not scrimp on fineries on the basis of general principle, but spent their money generously where it pleased them most. Which was why Aunt Wesma had decided, after reading an article on steeplechases in *Southern Living,* (our magazine of Martha Stewartish lifestyles below the Mason-Dixon line) that she might invest a little money in a steeplechase horse. When Aunt Wesma was a child her family had raised mules and Tennessee Walking Horses. Horses of the non-jumping variety had always been in her blood. She was ready to expand her interests.

And so it was decided that I would escort Uncle Hoyt and Aunt Wesma to their first steeplechase, so they could study Aunt Wesma's idea. I got VIP tickets for the event, and ordered a handsome picnic lunch from a local caterer. I packed wooden tray tables, linens, and colorful plates and glasses (the kind of Wal-Mart plastics that decorators call "festive," but only if used outdoors.) I had my snazzy little BMW washed, polished, and detailed. I was a young professional woman and a modern southern-belle hotshot, all the way.

I didn't stand a chance with Uncle Hoyt and Aunt Wesma. They arrived at my townhouse in their sparkling, cherry-red pick-up truck, a muscular and deluxe model with leather seats and state-of-the-art gizmos, including a booming CD player for Uncle Hoyt's George Jones collection.

"Oh, honey, you got the tickets for us; we couldn't let you do the food, too," Aunt Wesma insisted when I showed them my neatly packed wicker hamper. Uncle Hoyt slapped a hand on a huge blue ice-chest in his truck's bed. "We brung enough eats for us and the neighbors," he bragged. "Now, get yourself in the truck and let us show you a good time. That's all there is to it."

I was defeated and knew it. Trying to explain the world we were about to enter would only have insulted them. We drove out of my suburban enclave into the green rolling hills of the spring countryside, George Jones singing loudly on the truck's high-tech speakers, Uncle Hoyt driving with one hand and adjusting his cheek full of chewing tobacco with the other, Aunt Wesma catching me up on family gossip as she crocheted an orange afghan for a University of Tennessee nephew, and me gazing out the truck's passenger window with a worried headache between my brows. I did not want my favorite aunt and uncle to be humiliated.

The steeplechase was held in an enormous pasture; it resembled a modern medieval tournament with colorful tents scattered about. A white wooden announcer's booth rose from the center of the temporary steeplechase course, which was outlined in white wooden barricades and stacks of baled hay. Several thousand people had already arrived, channeled into outlying parking areas by stern off-duty state patrol officers hired for the event. They were setting up picnics on the grassy slopes surrounding the race course.

Thanks to my VIP tickets, we rolled past the less fortunate citizenry, with Uncle Hoyt nodding politely to the officers as if they'd granted him some special favor (which he was accustomed to getting, back in his own stomping grounds.) They directed us into a cordoned-off area in the middle of the course's infield, and we parked amongst a long line of fellow VIP vehicles. Prime viewing. Prime, period.

"Oh, my lord," Aunt Wesma sighed. "Will you look at this fancy crowd?"

We were surrounded by Rolls Royces, Jaguars, Mercedes, and enough luxury antique roadsters to start a car show. The owners—or their servants, because sometimes it was hard to tell—were setting up small personal compounds in front of their cars.

The silver Rolls beside us was the most lavish of all. Its tables were draped in fine white linen and anchored by silver candelabra or sterling vases bursting with fresh cut flowers. On them were feasts of fine finger foods, miniature quiches, fruits, fondues, and crudites, all on silver serving dishes or warming dishes. Circling these small banquets were teak or mahogany camp chairs, cushioned with tapestry pillows. A young man spread an oriental rug on the ground and set up his small feast. He was accompanied by several other well-dressed people, all of whom turned wide stares on us and the truck. I expected exotic women to appear at any moment, fanning our neighbors with ostrich feathers.

"Howdy," Uncle Hoyt called as he got out. They offered wan smiles and turned quickly to their gourmet nibbles and to glasses of champagne they poured from a tall bottle nestled in a silver ice bucket. Aunt Wesma snorted. "They'll get headaches, drinking outdoors like that before lunchtime."

"Good lord," Uncle Hoyt said, "I don't care about watching the hosses run. I just want to study this crowd of peacocks." We set about unpacking their ice chest, and within minutes had set up enough cold fried chicken, potato salad, baked beans and biscuits to feed an army, along with pound cake, pecan pie, and two jugs of iced tea. Aunt Wesma lowered the truck's tail gate, then spread her half-finished orange afghan across it like a tablecloth, and arranged the food, which was mounded in her best Tupperware. Next to it she set out paper plates, cups, and plastic utensils, all of it plain white, not festive. Uncle Hoyt unfolded three of his favorite striped lawn chairs, turned up a fresh George Jones CD on the truck's music system, then announced, "Time to take a walk to the barn," which was code for visiting the nearest toilet. After he wandered away, Aunt Wesma settled in a chair beside me with a napkin and a chicken leg.

The first sign of trouble came from the neighbor to our left. She was an elegant woman in silk pants and a sweater embroidered with horses jumping fences. Her tiny white poodle, wearing a jeweled collar, wandered over to Aunt Wesma and looked up eagerly at the fried chicken leg.

"Here, baby, you just help yourself," Aunt Wesma said to the poodle, then stripped the meat off and gave the miniature dog the leg bone. Aunt Wesma's family had raised hunting dogs for generations. Those hounds had prospered on table scraps. So would a poodle, she figured. I watched worriedly as the pint-sized dog dragged the bone next door.

The poodle's owner gasped. "What have you got! Oh!" She wrested the bone from the tiny dog's disappointed mouth and marched over to us, waving the illicit treat. "I'm sure you didn't mean any harm," she said to Aunt Wesma with condescending charm, "but I don't feed my dog garbage."

"Neither do I, honey," Aunt Wesma said with a placid smile. "Your poor little dog looks as hungry as a termite hunting for a plank to eat."

"I assure you, she'll get her own plate of gourmet dog food at lunch."

"That's nice, honey. But it ain't fried chicken."

"Please! This is not a stock car race!" The woman flung the leg bone on the grassy ground beside the truck. I glanced angrily around us, watching a flicker of smug smiles as others nibbled their caviar on toast points. The only exception was one dapper old man with a topknot of fine gray hair, which made him resemble a curious leghorn rooster with its head craned. He scowled at the poodle matron as she swept away.

"I'm sorry," I said to Aunt Wesma. "These people are uppity."

"They don't bother me none," she said with a laugh, and spooned potato salad on a paper plate.

"You can tell which people are fine and which just got money. Money can't make a silk purse out of a sow's ear."

A few minutes later a pair of well-dressed men walked by. "How quaint," one said loudly, and grinned at the truck. Not long after that, a pair of small children peered at us from behind the fender of a Rolls Royce. "Hillbillies," one whispered.

"Good morning, Sweetie Pies," Aunt Wesma called to them. They shrieked and ran away.

Aunt Wesma had a vulnerable nature when it came to children. Her unshakable good humor began to fade. "I reckon we don't fit in here," she said. "I ain't never been somewhere that the little folks were scared of me."

I said a half-dozen polite things to reassure her, at the same time growing angry over the stupidity of the silver-spoon society we'd entered. I fixed her a plate with another chicken leg on it, but she sat without eating.

"Ma'am?" a reedy voice called. It was the little old man nearby. He held a forlorn china plate dabbed with some sort of delicate yellow sauce and a pile of anemic-looking grilled shrimp. "Mighty fine looking bird leg you got there," he said to Aunt Wesma. To my surprise, his drawling, high-pitched voice was as country as sorghum syrup.

Aunt Wesma brightened. "You just come right over and help yourself," she replied. The little old man thumped his china plate down on a teak tray table and marched over to our camp, grinning. "Real folks," he proclaimed happily. "Just call me Buck. Glad to meet ya!"

We introduced ourselves and all shook hands,

and he pulled up a chair. Heads turned. People stared with new interest. When Uncle Hoyt returned he found Aunt Wesma and Buck jawing merrily while the elegant crowd inched closer, ears cocked and attitudes humbled.

Because Buck—his nickname—was a retired four-term state governor, one of the most notable politicians in the South.

This is the power of southern life, and the magic of sports. Even the odd ones like steeplechase can't keep us apart, and a sharing of southern soul food, uppity manners, and downhome honesty makes fans of us all.

THE REUNION

by Sandra Chastain

When archaeologists discover the missing arms of Venus de Milo, they will find she was wearing boxing-gloves.
—John Barrymore

My sister married a man named Robby who came from the mountains of Appalachia. When Sissy married Robby, he was an outsider. That means we didn't know his family; they weren't from our part of the country. But Granny, with whom we both lived, was willing to take him in. Tennessee folks couldn't be that different from the ones who lived in South Georgia, she reasoned.

But Robby just never made any attempt to fit in. He fancied himself an artist, a creative genius who was always just about to make it big. In the meantime, it was Sissy who made the living and Robbie who "created" paintings of something. We were never quite sure of what because, according to Robbie, what a person saw was a personal message the painting had for him or her. In each case, he insisted, the message was different. Granny said, "He'd've done better if he'd put a stamp on it and used it for writing paper."

I guess we're of a different time from Granny,

but enough of her philosophy sunk in that when trouble between Sissy and Robby came, it wasn't a surprise. After ten years and two children, the marriage was headed for divorce court. But a new family court law and a stern judge forced Sissy and Robby to see a counselor before he'd grant the divorce. The counselor insisted that, for the sake of the children, one last attempt at a reconciliation should be made. He thought the upcoming Thanksgiving holiday would provide the perfect opportunity.

That's how Sissy and the girls found themselves headed for Tennessee on a snowy Thanksgiving eve. Over the hills and through the woods took on a whole new meaning after six hours in a nine-year-old Ford with two cranky children, one adult anxiously trying to save his marriage while the other was killing it mile by mile. I told my sister not to go. But she thought she'd be able to hide in all the hurrah and not have to deal with Robby. They would have satisfied the counselor and she'd get out.

Her first mistake was consenting to the trip, her second in agreeing to go a day early, the day before Thanksgiving. By the time they arrived, all she wanted to do was eat and go to bed—in separate beds. But Robby's Grandma had invited her sister Bessie for dinner.

When Bessie didn't show up and didn't answer the phone, Sissy and Robby were sent to find out why. Her car was still in the drive, the house dark and the dead bolt lock firmly in place.

Robby, always willing to give up if a problem interfered with something he really wanted to do, was ready to forget about Bessie and do a little marital reminiscing in the back of the car—in the interest of reviving the marriage. Sissy, on the other hand, was not having any fooling around. It was the back seat of that car that got her into trouble in the first place.

The hour was late and she was already regretting that she'd let guilt over depriving her poor children of a father force her to make the trip. Investigating the rear of the house, she found a window in the utility room unlocked and climbed in. Turning on the lights, she made her way to the front door which she opened, then turned and found Bessie dead in the hallway. Heart attack, the doctor confirmed later that night.

At that point, Sissy had no idea that the burial would be delayed for days until all the family could gather, often from long distances and at great hardship. She didn't know that it would be a time when they'd laugh, gossip and visit while they committed the loved one to those hallowed halls of memory at whatever cost to their everyday lives, then stay on for a day or two to comfort the bereaved—and laugh, talk and visit some more.

This was an awakening to Sissy. Our irreverent family members have themselves cremated and their ashes sprinkled in various places around the world. If we wanted to go to the cemetery to pay our respects, we'd have to swim oceans, climb mountains, and dig in Granny's rose garden. That's where Gramps had his ashes scattered. "Might as well get some good out of 'em," he said before he went. Granny's roses have won the blue ribbon in the county fair every year since.

In Tennessee, Thanksgiving dinner plans were shelved immediately in lieu of the notifying and gathering of the family. Sissy, accepting that they'd have to stay an extra day, immediately offered her help—anything to pass the time and get through the ordeal.

Never did she expect to be given a list of thirty-six family members to call. And she certainly didn't expect that many of these people would have no phones; or that the numbers she would reach were neighbors and mountain stores that would send word of Bessie's passing. But when she was told that the day and time of the funeral would be decided "later," she knew that her hope to be on the road for home and marriage's end by Saturday was growing dim. Sissy put away her suitcases and her video camera. This was not an event she ever wanted to relive.

In the meantime, people came, some to stay and "help out," others to bring casseroles. By the end of the day, they had tuna casserole, potato and sausage casserole, squash casserole and finally a chicken casserole made from a rooster killed and stewed that afternoon.

The funeral home rushed over bringing folding chairs and wedged them in the living room, dining room and den. They put up book stands on pedestals by the doors where visitors could sign in, provided a white food record for the kitchen and a tasteful white and mauve notebook with gold embossed letters for the guests to sign. Robbie's mama was given a choice of three different kind of thank you notes she could choose from to express her appreciation for the casseroles. She picked one with a Bible verse and a pair of folded hands that looked more holy than the others.

Within thirty minutes of the discovery of the body, the local florist had opened up and delivered two pots of bronze mums and a pot of home-made vegetable soup to the house. The Women's Missionary Society brought the coffee urn from the church and plastic cups and spoons.

Sissy was finally informed, in hushed voices

away from the children, that the day and time of the funeral had to be decided on "later," not because of the weather—even though they were on the leading edge of an early winter blizzard—but because Bessie's boy was in Federal Prison for "some little thing" he'd done. And the authorities had to be reached over a holiday weekend and convinced to let him out for his mother's passing.

When the snow began to fall steadily, nine children ranging in age from six to ten transformed into raging maniacs intent on turning the furniture into Mt. Everest and their little hands and feet into mountain climbing equipment. There was no quieting them, nor, my sister discovered, separating her children from the heathens they called cousins. But it became her job to watch them while the others planned the funeral. What Bessie would be buried in became of paramount importance. The funeral director agreed to open on Thanksgiving Day so that they could select a casket.

The madness finally ended when a pallet for her children was made on the floor of the bedroom Sissy was to share with Robby. After an hour of, "this floor's hard," and "I want to go home" from the children and, "Can't you shut them up?" from Robby, Sissy seized the opportunity and planted their youngest in bed with Robby and herself on the hard, cold floor with their oldest daughter.

The next day brought more family and the realization that such a thing as viewing the body at the funeral home was tantamount to an appearance before the queen. Trousers could be worn if she hadn't brought Sunday clothes for herself and the girls, but running shoes and sweatshirts were "out of the question."

Sissy, already concerned about the state of their bank account, would have to go shopping. "I hope Robby brought a suit," his mama said. "He'll have to be a pall bearer."

"But he's a member of the family," Sissy argued, seeing the bank account dwindle farther. "I thought pall bearers were honored family friends." Her statement was ignored. It was obvious that her experience was as foreign to Robby's family as his family was to her.

"For goodness sakes, not here in the mountains. Members of each of the deceased's brother's and sister's family serve as honorary pall bearers. It's always been done that way."

Robby, standing behind his mother, was shaking his head. That desperate look said that he was ready to bolt, except this time he couldn't. This was his family, and he had to deal with them.

In the four-wheel drive someone volunteered for their use for a trek to Wal-Mart, Robby set off the first volatile argument of the Thanksgiving season. "I am not buying a suit and walking down that aisle carrying that coffin."

"Take it up with your mother," Sissy said, watching the snow swirl and wondering what this would do to their return trip in a certified clunker without tire chains.

"You'll have to tell her," he insisted. "Bessie was my favorite aunt. I'm too upset. She'll understand."

What Sissy understood was that Robby was wimping out. Nothing new about that.

On one point, he was saved. It was Thanksgiving. The Wal-Mart was closed. Sam Walton would never expect mountain folks to be away from their families on Thanksgiving. "But," Robbie told his mother, "it doesn't matter because I'm not going to do it."

Robby's mother cried. Robby went into his familiar nobody-understands-me silent mode, and the frenzy of family, food and children heightened. A second foray into town on Friday resulted in acceptable black jeans and white shirts for the children, a black dress for Sissy and shoes that none of them would ever wear again. And this was only for the "viewing." Robby refused to buy anything. "Fine," Sissy said. "It's your family."

The justice department agreed to release their prisoner for his mother's funeral on Sunday, but he'd be shackled because of whatever "little thing" he'd done, and would be discreetly escorted by a guard.

On Saturday morning Sissy was told that Robby absolutely had to have a suit and it was up to her to see that he got one. If they couldn't afford it, his mother would "go into her savings." There were six pall bearers and with Cousin Frankie in shackles there was nobody to take Robby's place in the funeral procession. By this time, Sissy would have slept with Hannibal Lector to get out of Tennessee. Using her most feminine wiles and a quicky in the bathroom, she talked Robby into going back to Wal-Mart. That's when the next disaster came. Since she'd enticed him into sex, he decreed that he expected her to forget about any more talk about divorce.

If Sissy had been in her right mind, she would have simply smiled and let Robby believe what he wanted. But too much family, food and togetherness had sapped her reason. She told him that this weekend had shown her if nothing else hadn't that they were definitely not compatible. Once they got through this funeral and back home, the marriage was over.

With that, Robby turned the vehicle back to the house, invited his wife of ten years to get out and announced dramatically, in front of a newly arriving family member, "Since you don't want to have any part of me, you can find your own way back home. I'm out of here."

Now Sissy and her children were stranded in what might as well be a land of foreigners, in the middle of a blizzard with no car and no money, facing a steady diet of casseroles.

"He'll come back," his Mama said. "These things just happen when we're grieving. He knows how humiliating it would be for us not to have him carrying poor Bessie's body into the church. Robby's just...delicate, always has been."

This was the description of a man who ran five miles a day and refused to eat meat. Robby didn't leave Tennessee because he was delicate. He left because he was a coward, and he didn't return. Sissy grew desperate. She couldn't even call me for I was in Florida with my husband's family. By the time they were to leave for the church on Sunday afternoon, Robby hadn't returned. His mother was having heart palpitations over trying to keep the little ones from seeing poor Frankie in chains for fear they'd be scarred for life. "We'll just have to put off the funeral until Robby gets back," she finally said. "I won't bury my own sister without filling the family slot."

"What," Sissy asked, "would you do if you only had single girls?"

A look of total astonishment swept over her face. "But that's never happened. And, if it had, I

136

guess one of the girls would have to fill in."

"Fine," Sissy agreed. "Tell me what to do."

And so it was decided that, if that's what it took, Sissy, on her way out of the family, would be the first female pall bearer in history. She'd get the woman in the ground and she and the girls would walk home if that's what it took. Just as they started out the door for the church, Robby's mom stopped Sissy with a teary request. "I saw you had your camera. Will you videotape the funeral? I mean, some folks will make pictures at the grave site, but a tape would be a splendid memory of Bessie's passing. Just don't get Frankie's feet in the picture."

And so it was that as her last family duty, Sissy carried Bessie's coffin into the church with her left hand and taped the proceeding with her right.

As it turned out, she managed to hitch a ride on a plane filled with marching-band members on their way home from an appearance at Macy's Thanksgiving Parade. By that time, Robby was well on his way to Reno where he eventually found a woman who appreciated his art, and my sister's marriage ended.

But every Thanksgiving Sissy still gets a thank-you note from her ex-husband's mother. It seems that in addition to women pall bearers, my sister is responsible for another family tradition. Every year, after turkey and dressing, the family gathers to watch the tape of Bessie's passing. Frankie's still in jail—another "little something" he did, and Robby's new wife refuses to cross the Mississippi.

Sissy's video of Bessie's passing is the only way all the family can be together.

GRANDPAPA'S GARDEN

by Deborah Smith

Gardening is an instrument of grace.
—May Sarton

The southern soil knows the heart. It remembers, it cries, or it can sit in stony, dry silence when its passions tell it to sleep. In the garden, in the field, in the window box or the clay pot, our roots grow deep and our leaves unfurl with stoic hope.

Grandpapa's roses bloomed their prettiest the spring he died. They mourned his passing and celebrated his life along with the rest of us, a little bewildered by the invisible change of seasons, their roots shaken, but sturdy overall, thanks to Grandpapa's careful nurturing. The roses, like us, had been established in rich earth. Grandpa, after all, was a gardening man.

He cultivated the roses in memory of Grandmother, who died years ago. In his loneliness he sought solace through the one thing she had loved nearly as much as him and their children: Flowers. Before her death he claimed to be a no-nonsense man, a man who put his values in livestock and paying crops, but after she was gone he learned the power of temporary beauties. And so in her honor he created a scarlet red rose that grew as wildly as a long-limbed child, twining over fences and peeking from hedgerows with dozens of brilliant blooms, each big enough to fill a tea cup. The rose won many awards, which he displayed in Grandmother's china cabinet along with her most delicate chintz plates, a porcelain celebration of living art.

Grandpapa took on the look of a hunched garden sprite in his old age; he could frighten a child at first glance, but children always noticed his eyes right away. Warm and blue and laughing, they were as friendly as old-fashioned petunias, and then the children smiled at him. He had large, strong hands, jug ears, and a frizz of gray hair that had once been coal black. He had a craftsman's logic, a poet's judgment, and at heart was most at home among heavy farm equipment and men who spit tobacco. He had four loyal brothers, all younger than he, and so it was Grandpapa who inherited the family farm, a sprawling mountain home, and the unspoken title of family patriarch.

The furrows of his life had been turned and replanted many times; he had harvested more than one kind of crop, and some said he was not much of a farmer because he couldn't abide too much of the same produce. He laughed and replied that it was a shame to bore the earth. And so one time he planted nothing but easy hay crops for a few years, so he'd have time to serve as mayor of our town after a tornado nearly wiped us off the face of the earth. He planted self-sufficient corn while he worked for the state agriculture department as an extension agent, during that era when an agent might still drive out to your barn and help you mend your tiller; he planted moody tomatoes while he sold tractors for a living, and had a fling with cabbage when he operated a bulldozer service.

He learned to farm from his father and his mother, and thus the urge to plant, grow, and harvest had borne in him many generations of know-how, an infinite progression of instincts for rain and sun. He snorted at newspaper horoscopes but could pinpoint the right phase of the moon for any seed. He chaired the county fair for two decades; he spoke his piece to governors and senators as president of the district farm co-op.

He killed a man in self-defense when he was twenty years old, stopping an armed robbery at the local service station. Then he never touched a gun again.

He chased every pretty girl in the county as a handsome young man, then upset them all when he found the perfect wife at a church reunion two counties over. He loved her faithfully, called her the best woman in the world, and together they raised children who came home regularly and loved them both, and grandchildren who learned a charmed, caterpillar's-eye view of the world among his flowers. His life was a tapestry so rich only his garden could do it justice. When the illness came he thought he would beat it; he tilled and planted between treatments, he spread the white specks of fertilizer like a man feeding chicks, talking to the earth as he fed it. He left us unexpectedly, with weeds still to be pulled, mulch to be spread, twigs to be pruned. Life and weeds, as a lesson to us, continued without him.

His death scared us, shook our faith in spring-time, sent us to our Bibles, our liquor cabinets, and our wisest friends. We were on unfamiliar ground; the sun too brilliant, the air so sweet it could wash tears from the eyes and bring a soul to kneel on the begging dirt. Peonies still bloomed, daisies and irises and daylillies and gladiolas sprang up as before, Queen Anne's Lace and Crown Vetch still found their sly way into the beds like uninvited guests depending on charm to ensure their welcome. Family and friends came as worshipers to take small cuttings from Grandpapa's roses, dividings from his mums, seeds from his poppies and columbines and other plants. They wanted the heirloom inspirations of the life he had lived so fully; they wanted his secret for happiness.

Yet when a distant relative died a few weeks later, superstitious old ladies whispered over their chicken-salad luncheons, "Death comes in threes." When a beloved young cousin announced her new pregnancy, we congratulated her but worried about portents and timing. She had miscarried three babies before this, and the doctors had warned her and her husband to stop trying. My cousin had listened with the best intentions, but life often takes root even when you try your hardest to give up hope.

She beamed with terrified happiness. We made her sit in a cushioned willow chair among the shade of old oaks each time the rest of us met to tend Grandpapa's garden. Through all the months that followed we kept his covenants, but we turned dark, worried eyes to the beloved young cousin, as she grew larger and paler through the summer and into the fall. It was never enough to wish for the best result;

141

you had to get out into your life's garden every day, working your rows, poking around your beds for signs of trouble, plucking out the weeds and spraying the insects before they sucked the life out of your courage. Aunts, uncles, brothers, sisters, and cousins met in endless consultations over birth, death, and crabgrass that year, working Grandpapa's garden, keeping our worries inside the borders of his fieldstone paths, pruning our fears as if they were blackberry briars.

In the crisp cold of October we raked the jewel-toned leaves and burned them in fat piles, taking comfort in their autumn incense, watching their smoke drift gently into the sky. The moon rose plump and yellow, a harvest moon, and with our ripening young cousin we carved jack o'lanterns from small pumpkins grown from plants Grandpapa had set out immediately after the last spring frost. He still lived; his season's handiwork had born fruit and all was well, so far, with this garden's memories.

Then November came, and with it the silver, iced dew, and the sun retreated. The ground in Grandpapa's garden grew still and bare, and we waited, we waited with held breath, in that quieting time of the year, when new life is hard to imagine. She began to suffer, our young cousin. Small ailments, and then larger ones, her time so close that we could feel the boy child move, defying the coming winter. We prayed that he dreamed of warm suns and gentle rains, that the promise of life could lure him safely into our arms.

On the coldest day of January, the doctors said his mother would not live through the night with him inside her. They opened her, they slipped him from her warmth, mewling and gasping, searching for the sunshine. Infinite dark hours followed. Many of us went to Grandpapa's garden during that eternal night. We were drawn helplessly to the rich, quiet heart of our family, speaking to God under the shadows along empty flower beds, and beside roses with bare vines.

She lived. Against all common sense and signs of the moon, she lived. And he lived, too, our new little boy, our next generation who would tend the garden. In the spring, when he had spent enough time with us to know how far his small hands might reach before ours reached out in response, I brought him a small offspring from Grandpapa's roses, bearing one brilliant scarlet bloom, sacred and alive. He touched it in velvet wonder, and smiled his great-grandpapa's smile.

UNCLE CLETE'S BELL

by Nancy Knight

The best part of marriage is the fights.
The rest is merely so-so.
—Thornton Wilder

Death is serious business. Everybody knows that. And when somebody dies, people do the dangdest things. They may start to squabble over who gets what or who the deceased loved best—or even worse. And nothing will stop them. Almost. Sometimes it takes an extraordinary event to make folks come to their senses.

When Mama's brother, Clete, passed away, we went to the mortuary to view the body and visit with family. Just after sunset, Mama, my sister Joyce, and I paraded into the old Victorian home that served as a funeral parlor. Mama had baked a chocolate-nut pound cake for Aunt Bett, so I took it over to her car and placed it on the front seat floorboard. Mama always took her special chocolate-nut pound cake when somebody died.

The parking lot full of cars told me to expect to see a lot of my cousins and old friends, and maybe a few people I didn't know. Funeral gatherings are huge occasions where people unite to talk about the dearly departed and catch up on the gossip and news. I

144

always looked forward to these occasions, except when the deceased was a relative of mine, of course.

As a child, I'd always loved going to Uncle Clete's and Aunt Bett's. They had a huge farm with lots of exciting places to play. Uncle Clete and Aunt Bett had seven children: Junior, Billy Joe, Jack, Sammy, Wayne, Rose, and Violet. What fun we had exploring the farm buildings, playing make believe in the woods, sliding down the banks of the red-clay ditches eroded by heavy rains, riding pigs, and sneaking down to the creek for a swim. Those were the days!

We were all grown up now, married with our own children. Since I lived out of town and didn't get home often, I was eager to see everyone again, to remember old times together.

Hicks Funeral Parlor boasted hardwood floors, shining and slick beneath my leather clad feet. Managing somehow to walk without slipping, I entered the first room used for the public. All the relatives were gathered there.

All five of Uncle Clete's boys had been married more than once. In fact, some of them had been married more than three times. They were all honest, hard working folks, but they just couldn't make their marriages work. Or maybe they were just following their daddy's example.

I spotted Junior's first wife, Mattie. We hugged and I chatted with her and her girls before moving on. We still had a lot of relatives to visit with. At that point, I glanced around the room and noted just how many wives and ex-wives were assembled around the perimeter. There were plenty of them, perched on the edge of reproduction Duncan Phyfe sofas and Queen Anne chairs. And none of them looked too happy to be seated in the same room with their former husbands, other ex-wives, and current wives. The phrase "if looks were daggers" was made for this occasion. It quickly became apparent to me that one of the reasons, besides genuine grief of course, the women were here was to see their predecessors and their precursors, and perhaps, to get in a few barbs.

We made the rounds, talking to various and sundry aunts, uncles, cousins, second cousins, third cousins' spouses, and ex-spouses. I was thoroughly confused just trying to remember who belonged to whom. We are a big family, and the complicated second and third marriages didn't help any. I've got more branch-water kin than baby frogs after a summer rain. I talked to Sammy's latest ex-wife, cooed at Jack's new baby boy, and then chatted with Billy Joe's oldest daughter, who happily showed me her engagement ring. With a quick glance at a roomful of failed marriages, I offered her my best wishes. The teenage girl prattled on and on about her wedding plans while I smiled and nodded. As soon as possible, I moved on.

My cousin, Sammy, came in. He lives in New York and has been trying to make it big for years. Thus far, his major accomplishment has been as assistant stage manager for an off-off-off-Broadway theater for little money and no fame. He and I share the "label" of black sheep of the family. Not that we do anything bad, but we are just the most interesting and, maybe, a little outlandish. So we have a lot in common. We hugged, kissed, and talked for a while. He'd just flown in and hadn't even seen his mama, so we vowed to keep in touch and drifted apart.

Mama introduced me to Junior's current wife, Sally Faye, a pretty waif-like creature with huge brown eyes and wispy brown hair. I'd never met her, but tried to make pleasant conversation. After all, her new father-in-law had just died. To my surprise, she started right off explaining that she and Junior were thinking about separating. My surprise turned to astonishment as she continued. God had called Junior to the ministry and had given him Bobbi Sue to take care of. I didn't know exactly who Bobbi Sue was, but I assured Sally Faye that everything would work out. She just needed to be patient.

"Men," I explained in my most comforting voice, "sometimes get the craziest notions. He'll come to his senses pretty quick, I'm sure." I wasn't sure at all, but it was the best I could offer in the way of reassurance on such short notice.

It occurred to me that we frequently speak in platitudes. "Oh, he'll come to his senses." And they never do. Or, "I declare, that's the prettiest baby I ever saw." We say that even if the infant in question would draw a blister on an outhouse from a hundred yards away. "Brides are always beautiful, aren't they?" We have lots of those, none of which are true most of the time, but we say them anyway.

Everything seemed to be going smoothly, up to that point. Keep uttering those tried and true phrases, I told myself. "He's just going through a mid-life crises. Tell him to buy himself a new truck and he'll get over it."

And then Junior arrived—with his arm draped around a girl half his age. I knew immediately that I was looking at Bobbi Sue. The new girlfriend. Blonde and beautiful, clad in a black sheath skirt and spaghetti strap halter that boasted only a string tie at the neck and waist in the back, she looked like the

147

latest cover girl for *Cosmo*. I'd been expecting some-body who might grace the cover of a magazine like *Tractor Backing Gazette*. My words to wife number two (or three, I don't remember which) just floated there in the air between us like the smell of a dead skunk on a hot summer night. I met her embarrassed gaze and shrugged. What else could I do?

The sweet expression on Junior's present wife's face changed from apple dumpling sweet to green persimmon bile. A nasty little thought entered my mind. I could imagine one of these women whipping out a gun and opening fire on the other ex-wives or present wives. Stranger things have happened. I excused myself, muttering that there were people I hadn't yet talked to, and rushed over to Mama who was discussing diaper rash with Jack's wife.

I hurried Mama and Sis along, not wanting to witness the possible bloodshed. We sped on through the rest of the current wives and ex-wives into the next room. (With great relief.)

The coffin was in that room. Uncle Clete had been married twice. He and Aunt Bett had divorced not long before Great-Granny Tolleson died. He married Aunt Connie a few years later, but they hadn't been getting along too well, according to Mama. They had been separated and planning to divorce. But the clincher was yet to come. Soap opera writers only wish for material like this, I thought. Uncle Clete had been planning to re-marry Aunt Bett. Confused? I was, but somehow I liked the idea of them getting back together. Of course, now that could never happen.

I'm not too sure that Uncle Clete understood all of that either. He was a man with little formal education, but a world of knowledge from the school of hard knocks and life. He was a man of the land, a man who could coax Blossom into giving an extra quart of milk. His favorite pig, Porcina, had won more ribbons at the state fair than any other in the history of South Carolina. He understood life and enjoyed living it.

But there was that shiny, pale green coffin with Uncle Clete, looking all peaceful and serene, as if he were asleep. Tied to his finger was a string attached to a little bell—a precaution, in the way of a long-standing tradition, in case he wasn't really dead. I reckon that's a practice that has fallen out of favor, what with better medical technology these days. We pretty well know for sure a body's dead nowadays, but that wasn't always the case.

In years past, when a body was buried, the bell was left above ground for five days—just in case the "deceased" wasn't really dead. If that was the case, the "deceased" would wiggle his hand and shake the bell. The cemetery attendant would rescue the victim. That little bell reportedly saved several lives over the years.

I always cry at these times and this was no exception. I really loved Uncle Clete. He was so much fun when I was growing up. And here he was, about to be buried. With tears in my eyes, I told stories of how he'd bounced me on his knee when I was a girl, pulled my pony-tail when I was a teenager, and how he'd teased me when I decided to get married.

I went to my Aunt Bett, since I was closer to her than Aunt Connie. I hugged her, shed a few tears with her, and told her everything would turn out all right. She would just have to take each day as it came. I said all the things you say to people whose spouses have passed away. "He looks so natural doesn't he?"

She smiled, dabbed at the corner of her eye with an embroidered hanky, and nodded. "Looks like he might wake up any minute."

"He really does," I said. He really didn't, though. He'd died of a sudden heart attack and wasn't found for nearly two days. The thick make-up on his face made him look anything but natural to me.

"You know, he had left that other woman." Aunt Bett gestured with her head toward the other end of the coffin. "We were planning to remarry."

And then I noticed something peculiar. Aunt Bett was sitting at Uncle Clete's head and Aunt Connie was sitting at his feet. And they were glaring at each other with enough venom to kill a prize bull. Guns in those big purses, maybe? Nah. They were too civilized for that.

Aunt Connie's blanket of red and white carnations lay on the coffin. After all, they weren't divorced yet, so it was her place to buy the coffin blanket.

Behind Aunt Bett stood a wreath the size of an eighteen-wheeler's tire. Huge. Humongous. I swear, the President of the United States never placed a wreath so big on the Tomb of the Unknown Soldier. I stared.

Draped across those yellow and gold football mums was a five inch wide sash of yellow satin ribbon. Printed in letters of three inch gold glitter were the words, "I still love you."

I looked at Aunt Bett and then at Aunt Connie. I knew the reason for the daggers in the air between them. Jealousy over a dead man.

The stare-down escalated as the afternoon wore

on. Aunt Connie muttered something about a pretentious and gaudy display. Aunt Bett heard, deliberately reached over and folded the coffin blanket halfway down, and the fight was on.

The verbal barrage began in earnest. At that point, I realized that words might not satisfy either of my aunts. Where is a good platitude when you need one, I asked myself as I backed away from the coffin.

Heads turned; eyes riveted on the two silver-haired women standing at the ends of the coffin yelling at each other over Uncle Clete's body. Daughters-in-law—former, current, and future—drifted into the parlor to see who was causing the ruckus. They began to take sides and squabble among themselves. I watched, mesmerized, as the shouting rose to a crescendo and evolved into a hollering contest. Glancing at Uncle Clete, I noticed something different about him. He appeared to be frowning. Lines had materialized on his forehead and around his mouth. No, he was definitely scowling. Hadn't there been a look of peace on his face moments before?

Accusations flew back and forth. The two combatants approached each other like two mongrels circling a bone. A little shoving broke out. I tried to break it up, but got jostled out of the way. There was no stopping this riot now.

I grabbed Mama by the arm and dragged her toward the door. I just knew a shoot-out was about to occur, and I didn't want to become a witness or a victim. I glanced again at Uncle Clete, knowing that this peace-loving man would hate such a display. Again, his appearance surprised me. The look on Uncle Clete's face had certainly changed to one of great displeasure. It was a look I'd seen when we'd inadvertently let the dogs into the chicken coop one afternoon.

As we approached the door, the battle reached its zenith. Dour-faced morticians, frantic sons, sobbing daughters, and confused daughters-in-law tried to separate the women who were now swinging freely at each other. But the poor men didn't fare so well. Aunt Bett slugged the senior funeral director, and Aunt Connie knocked the preacher off his feet with her huge purse.

Mama, Joyce, and I hovered near the door, watching in amazement at the full-scale hysteria sweeping the room. Nobody seemed capable of being just a by-stander—except for us, that is. Not even Uncle Clete. His displeasure had escalated to anger.

Just then, a sound brought fists to a stop in mid-air. Quiet rippled across the room until every voice fell silent. The only sound was a vigorously jangling bell.

Aunt Bett swooned in mid-swing, only to be caught by Junior who boasted a fresh black-eye. Aunt Connie's jaw hung open as she gaped at the coffin and the still-tinkling bell. Mama fainted dead-away. Sis and I helped her to a chair as the other women began to drift apart, shame faced.

We never knew what caused the bell to ring just then. A post-mortem spasm? A combatant bumping against the coffin in the confusion? Perhaps it's best if we never know. There's no telling how many wives and ex-wives—not to mention innocent bystanders—might have been killed if Uncle Clete's bell hadn't clanged when it did.

Just before the shooting began.

SWEET TEA

by Debra Dixon

*Marriage is like buying something you've been admiring for a
long time in a shop window...you may love it when you get
home but it doesn't always go with everything else in the house.*
—Jean Kerr

In the South you grow up steeped in tradition.
It's not that you find the South particularly
quaint or interesting. You simply have no choice.
By the time Miss Eulayla Overstreet, or her equiva-
lent, places the metronome-from-hell on the family
piano, you know four very important things that will
shape your life. You know who your people are, where
the homeplace is, and that you will never, ever like
the piano.

You also know precisely how much sugar to put
in a gallon of tea.

True sweet tea is a sublime syrupy DNA test
for family identity. You either belong to the syrup
subset of Southerners or you belong to the carpetbaggers who moved down from up North. Sweet is
sweet, and you can't cheat. No hostess of any stature
would be caught dead sweetening her iced tea at the
table.

More than once I've asked myself how a modest beverage gained so much power. The simple answer is that sweet tea is the dividing line between *us* and *them*. But I didn't truly understand how sharp that line was until the summer I graduated from college. I invited my fiancé's parents down South to meet my kinfolks.

To paraphrase a famous Yankee: It was a day that would live in infamy.

❂❂❂

Five o'clock had come and gone, but I still stood frozen in front of my closet, wondering which outfit would please my mother, fiancé, and my future mother-in-law.

"Shelby! Shelby Lynn! Shelby Lynn Jackson!" The screech reaching up the stairs, through the cracks and crevices of our old house and into my bones was unmistakable.

Aunt Claree.

Aunt Claree was Daddy's brother's widow, a blue-haired harridan of impeccable pedigree. The nicest thing I could say about Aunt Claree was that on a sober day, her stare could peel paint off the sides of completely weathered barns. Any hope I had of surviving the evening evaporated.

I closed my eyes and grabbed the first article of clothing I touched. The hem of a bright blue, casual-yet-Sunday-go-to-meeting dress had barely covered my butt on its way down to my knees when Claree stuck her head in.

"Lordamercy, girl. The very idea! Do not be taking all day primping when you know the family's

154

got company coming. Your poor Mama could use some help down there! It's not her boyfriend's family we're trying to impress, you know."

I bit my lip. It was either that or ask Aunt Claree why she wasn't down there helping Mama, especially since she hadn't been invited to supper. Instead, I stupidly substituted the next thought that crossed my dim-witted brain. "Oh, my goodness. I didn't know you'd been released!"

The paint-peeling stare was her only reply. Impossibly, the abnormally thin line of her mouth narrowed further. Retribution hovered in the air like the promise of rain after a streak of heat lightning.

I was going to pay for that slip of the tongue. How and when were yet to be determined, but Claree Jackson did not forgive a person for pointing out the truth. Her little visits to the Happy Trails Substance Abuse Center were never discussed using terms like treatment, release or dependency. Oh, no...Aunt Claree visited a spa. Aunt Claree needed some rest to rejuvenate. Aunt Claree went on spiritual retreats.

The simple, unvarnished truth was that Aunt Claree could suck down more alcohol between breakfast and lunch than any three church deacons on a weekend bender.

Without another word, Claree withdrew her head and shut the door firmly. Not so firmly as to be accused of slamming the door, but firmly enough to make her point and put the fear of God in me. Hell hath no fury like Aunt Claree in a snit.

Briefly, I considered calling Ian at the hotel and breaking off our relationship. If I'd thought I had a chance in hell of catching him, I would have given it a shot.

Instead I shoved my feet into a pair of sandals, sprinted down the back stairs to the kitchen, and put my faith in Mama's ability to run interference with Aunt Claree.

Mama is one of a dying breed—the Southern woman who can simultaneously prepare mass quantities of food, plan a church bazaar, set the table, discipline a grandchild, sew on a missing button, and swat the flies that sneaked inside every time we opened the back door to check Uncle Skeeter's barbecue technique.

All without breaking a sweat.

Southern women are scary. Even to me, and I grew up exposed to their supernatural powers. All that exposure has made me overly sensitive to the fact that the powers seemed to have skipped a generation in my family. However, I had been given a full-measure of social grace and a fairly well-developed survival instinct. I figured a compliment wouldn't hurt in an emergency.

I plastered a smile on my face and stepped into a kitchen filled with the aromas of simmering field peas, snap beans, and the lingering scent of baked apples. "Hmm...smells wonderful. What can I do to help?"

Before my compliment had time to find its mark, typhoid Claree sauntered into the kitchen from the direction of the dining room. "We've got it under control, sweetie. I wouldn't want you to ruin that pretty dress. Wherever did you get it? Not in town surely. Sissy Abbott doesn't sell rayon."

Rayon.

I looked down and realized I'd grabbed a rayon and poly blend dress out of the closet. Mama would not be happy.

Mama was a Martin by birth, and the Martins had always been staunch supporters of local industry. Nell Martin Jackson considers cotton to be politically correct and morally superior. Nell considers every rayon purchase I make to be a direct act of treason against the delta farmers.

Her daddy had raised cotton and, according to her, when the family lost the homeplace, it was a direct result of Northern industrial textile treachery. Oh, we still called the two thousand acres of bottomland over near the county line our homeplace. Hell, half the county still called it the Martin place. We just didn't own a piece of paper that said it belonged to us anymore. Even the tiniest reminder made Mama tear up quicker than a baby sucking hot milk.

I smiled lamely, considered torture for Claree, and braced for Mama's reaction.

She was up to her elbows in flour and chicken pieces. She adhered strictly to the traditional Martin recipe—each piece individually dipped in an egg/milk/seasoning concoction and rolled in flour. Twice. Still, she whipped around, a dripping breast in each hand, and gasped at me. "Oh for heaven's sake, Shelby! This is not the time to make a statement about your independence. You may not care about the Southern economy, but this is a family event. What will the McClarens think of us if we don't think enough of ourselves to protect our own heritage?"

In one horrifying moment I realized that the quirks and peculiarities a person acquired growing up Southern would be concentrated around tonight's supper table. On display like a traveling museum exhibit.

However, now was not the time to tell Mama that I was rapidly coming to believe lunacy was my heritage. Nor was I going to tell her that I'd be happy if the McClarens worst fear of me as a daughter-in-law was my disloyalty to the South. I was suddenly afraid that after tonight the McClarens were going to worry about the possibility of mentally defective grandchildren.

A little splinter of guilt at those thoughts lodged itself in my heart. These were my people—Mama, Claree, Uncle Skeeter, my brother Little Will (who was six foot three) and his wife and Tray. Everyone who'd be at the supper table loved me in their own way. Most loved me unconditionally. With the exception of Aunt Claree. Judging from the calculating expression on her face, she felt something unconditional for me at the moment, but I was fairly certain it wasn't love.

My people.

How could I tell Mama that a rayon dress wasn't tonight's problem? Or that I was afraid the McClarens would take one look at my gene pool and go screaming into the night? I couldn't. So, I lied.

"You know Ian's mama manages that chain of department stores. This was one of their dresses. They were overstocked, and she had Ian bring me one."

Mama thought for a minute. She used her forearm to brush a lock of silver-blonde hair out of her face and finally allowed, "Oh. Well. I suppose you had to wear it."

Claree snorted and reached for the big, rounded and hand-hammered aluminum pitcher we used for tea. "Well then, Nell, you might as well get used to Christmas alone. If Shelby worries so much about that woman's opinion before she's even married the son, you can bet she'll be at the McClaren supper table every holiday after the wedding!"

"Shut up, Claree." The words were as crisp and final as any I'd ever heard Mama utter to my aunt.

They'd never been the closest of sisters-in-law, not even after Daddy died and they could have bonded in widowhood. At best they'd always had an uneasy truce that recognized Claree's greater claim to the title of Jackson matriarch by dint of a ten-year age difference. Claree might be ten years older, but Mama didn't take advice about her kids from women who hadn't raised their own children.

In that one arena, Claree would never be her equal, and Mama knew it. "Now, why don't you make that tea if that's what you came in here to do? And, Shelby, stop standing there and answer the door since Little Will, Tammy, and Tray are in the back with Uncle Skeeter."

No door bell had rung, but I didn't question her; I started for the door. Mama had a sixth sense about company. A down right spooky sense really. While "mother's intuition" might explain the extra places already set when I had arrived with uninvited supper guests as a teenager, I had no explanation for why she always just happened to have the preacher's favorite banana pudding when he dropped in. Or an already-bagged donation if Shirley from the Goodwill stopped by to chat.

Given Mama's track record, I not only headed for the door, I gave the place a last minute once-over. On my way through the dining room, I inspected the Blue Willow china and straightened Granny Ida's serving pieces. Mama had cleared off the oak buffet in preparation for "food overflow." We'd need it.

She had every eye on the stove going. Pots warming between the eyes. Food in the oven. Food in the microwave, refrigerator, and on the grill. And catfish frying in the kettle out back.

She'd been cooking for three days; we'd be eating for three weeks. It was no surprise to me how Southerners survived the depression. We had a history of stockpiling food "just in case."

In the living room I straightened a couple of doilies on the back of a tapestry rocker and tried to imagine what the room would look like if I'd never seen it.

Good furniture. Mostly oak. Cluttered with original craft projects of Martha Stewart caliber. Except these craft projects had been inherited from relatives through the years.

Apparently Mama had never met a doily she didn't like. Doilies were everywhere. On top of and on each shelf of the curved glass curio cabinet. On every piece of furniture except the sofa, which was normally covered with a ratty old blanket to protect the fabric from Leroy's muddy paw prints. At least someone had thought to replace the blanket with one of our better patchwork quilts.

The door bell rang as I gave one last "fluff" to the garden flowers on the end table.

I've always considered answering that door an act of faith and bravery. Sort of like taking a bullet in battle because someone had to take the point. I plastered a smile on my face and approached the door to welcome Ian and my future in-laws. Their voices carried right through the wood.

In the South, it's not eavesdropping if people

talk loudly enough for you to hear through walls and doors. At least that's the rule in our family.

"I can't stand it, Ian. That porch swing would go for at least eight hundred at Stella's gallery. I can't believe they'd leave it out here in the weather. Anyone could just unhook it and steal it!"

A snort escaped me. Steal it? We'd tried to sell it in three yard sales and couldn't get five dollars for it. The swing needed a coat of paint; it squeaked; and it was older than dirt. Somehow, just knowing that Ian's mother wasn't the incredibly sophisticated woman I'd built up in my mind gave me some hope. I flung open the door.

And had the stuffing kicked right out of me.

The most gorgeous woman I had ever seen stood in front of me. Perfectly applied makeup. Slender. A watermelon-colored silk suit. Pumps to match. Short moussed hair. And a smile that must have cost more than my college education.

For the first time in my life, I mentally thanked my mama for relentlessly drilling social responses into me. Instinct took over or I couldn't have managed to form words. "Mrs. McClaren, hello and welcome. I'm just so glad you could join us."

She had one of those smiles that didn't quite warm her gaze or her voice. She glanced at Ian. "I didn't have much choice did I? Ian seems to have made his decision, and there's no talking him out of it."

"Not in this lifetime." Ian did have a smile that warmed his gaze, which was much too familiar in front of his mother. I could have strangled him.

"Yes, well." Mrs. McClaren shifted her gaze back to me. "So sorry, Shelby, dear. My husband was called back to New York. I hope that doesn't upset your little dinner party, and that your parents won't mind."

I stepped back from the door and wrestled with an age-old social dilemma: embarrass the poor woman now or wait for someone else to embarrass her later. I chose now. "I'm sure Mama will manage. She's had a bit of practice. Daddy died two years ago."

"Oh, then perhaps it is best that Everett had to return."

That didn't make much sense, but I wasn't going to ask how not seeing Everett would make Mama feel any better about Daddy's death. I was beginning to realize that my family was odd in a way that I could understand. Ian's would take some getting used to.

The whole conversation might have headed for safer ground if my nephew Tray hadn't come careening up the porch and barreled into all of us on his way inside.

"That damn dog is after me again!"

Tray is five.

The damn dog is a three-legged black and tan coonhound.

Tray's left butt cheek was hanging out of his blue jeans and there was no sign of a hip pocket. A shred of underwear trailed down the back of his thigh. Mrs. McClaren paled visibly and had the look of someone who'd been unexpectedly accosted by a homeless person. With good reason.

Leroy had greeted her just as he would have a new dog—by planting his nose in her crotch.

While Ian grabbed for Leroy's collar, I caught Tray the only way anyone had ever been able to stop Tray on a rampage. I grabbed a handful of hair before he got out of reach. In the split second of silence that followed the capture of dog and kid, I realized I was an unwilling participant in a scene from the *Illustrated Guide to Murphy's Law.*

I've always had a fairly well developed sense of the ridiculous. And some situations are just inherently funny. This was not one of them. When I saw the dog slobber stain on the front of Mrs. McClaren's silk skirt, I figured there was nothing worse Claree could do to me than what Murphy had already arranged.

There is a great deal of peace in hitting rock bottom.

When Tray squirmed, I transferred my grip to his arm without taking my eyes off Ian's mother. "I am so sorry, ma'am."

"No, it's...okay...really. I love...dogs." Her tone suggested that Leroy might not fit her definition of a dog—or anyone else's. She fished a tissue out of her tiny black purse and brushed distastefully at the wet spot. Ian—bless his heart—tried to lighten the moment by tousling Tray's hair.

"Whoa, pal. Tell us what you had in your pocket."

"Nothin'." Tray had the grace to look away when he lied.

Unfortunately he looked at Mrs. McClaren's skirt and giggled. Fortunately, Mama appeared in the doorway. She had never seemed more like the cavalry. She welcomed Ian to the family with a hug and introduced herself to Ruth McClaren.

"Now, why don't we go inside? I'm sorry your husband couldn't come, Mrs. McClaren. We've so looked forward to meeting Ian and you. While I finish up in the kitchen, you might like to freshen up in the bathroom? Then you can meet the rest of the family." With graceful motions and simple questions, she herded us inside, made the incident disappear and found time to ask Tray where his Daniel Boone cap was as she dragged him toward the kitchen.

In no more than the blink of an eye, Ian and I were alone with a coonhound and a case of the giggles. But before we could grab a hug and a kiss, his mother was back in the room, making a beeline for the sofa.

"It is! Oh, my. Now this is lovely." She smoothed the quilt's binding edge and then flipped a corner over to see the backing. Or the stitching.

"Mother collects quilts." Ian reached for my hand and rolled his eyes. "She's mad about them."

"Yes. I love them. It was about the only way Ian could convince me to come down here. He promised me quilts."

I stiffened at the obvious insult. Ian seemed oblivious, even when I pulled my hand from his.

"How old is this one?" Mrs. McClaren demanded.

"Old. You'll find pieces of Union and Confederate uniforms in it. Taken from uniforms of Jackson men when they came home. I think the woman who made it called it The Ties That Bind."

"This quilt?" She straightened excitedly as she pointed.

That was all the invitation Leroy needed. He pulled away from Ian, loped a few ungainly three-legged steps and launched himself squarely into the middle of Mama's sofa.

"Oh my God! Get him off!"

I scrambled for his collar. "No joke. Mama just washed that quilt. She'll kill him."

You'd have thought I slapped the woman. "You wash this quilt? In a washing machine?"

Aunt Claree slammed down a bowl on the dining room table and—since she'd been eavesdropping—answered for me. "Only when fools encourage the dog to sprawl on it." She stood in the archway and ran her eyes over Ian and his mother. "I'm Claree Jackson. Shelby's aunt."

And I'm dead.

"Ruth McClaren." She extended her hand like a man. When Claree only raised an eyebrow, Ruth dropped her hand and asked. "Do you have any idea what this quilt is worth?"

"Not as much as it was before the dog rolled on it."

Ian and I exchanged she's-your-relative-you-fix-it looks, but neither of us wanted the job. Coward that I was, I pretended I had to scoot Leroy out the front door. The house was well set back from the road, but I waited to be sure he ambled around to the backyard and stopped only long enough to urinate on his favorite mint patch at the corner of the house.

By the time I'd run out of my dog-watching excuse, Ruth and Claree were fast on the way to becoming life-long enemies. This visit was going downhill much too quickly. Ian looked desperate, and we still had Little Will, Tammy and Uncle Skeeter to introduce to Ruth. I honestly thought I had prepared Ian for my family, but he looked like a man suddenly presented with an electrified obstacle course.

"Let me get this straight," Ruth told Claree. "You have more of these quilts? Quilts that are seventy or even a hundred years old...and you use them everyday."

Claree sniffed. "Wouldn't be much good to us if we didn't. I don't know what you folks do when it's cold but we kind of like to cover up here in the South."

"Okay!" I clapped my hands with exaggerated enthusiasm. "What say we go out back and you can meet Uncle Skeeter? That'll be a treat. He's eighty-six, and won't let anyone else use the grill because none of us have killed a Nazi."

Neither woman responded to my invitation, but Ruth politely followed when my glare at Ian got his feet moving. As we passed the kitchen, Mama waved away our offers of help but told us not to dawdle since the tomatoes would be ready soon. Ruth looked appalled at the amount of frying pans on the stove. I heard her whisper to Ian, "Whatever you do, don't stop moving. These people will fry you."

Ian smiled, and I was surprised to find I didn't like it one bit. Sure, only a few minutes earlier I had been rolling my eyes at the "overflow" buffet, but questioning the quantity wasn't the same as maligning the quality. Or the variety. Mama certainly hadn't gone overboard frying things. We were only having fried chicken, fried corn, fried catfish, fried gizzards and livers, and fried green tomatoes. She certainly wasn't frying the pickles, the ice cream or the biscuits. She hadn't fried the pork chops, the okra, the squash or the eggplant.

Maybe Ian should have prepared me for his mother.

It was an effort to unfold my arms from my midsection and try one more time to like Ruth. Somehow I knew she'd prefer to be called Ruth, not Mom, and that was another strike against her.

Against Ian.

Ruth's superior gaze swept the property as we approached the concrete pad and the group of people huddled around a steel drum grill and the fish kettle. Her interest finally settled on Mama's well-tended garden patch. "I can't believe your mother has time to garden like this, Shelby. Are these organically grown?"

Uncle Skeeter cackled. "Daft woman. This is the South. Damn bugs are big enough to carry off suckling pigs, and you expect Nell could grow tomatoes that size without pesticide?"

"Silly of me I'm sure, but I'm not intimately acquainted with bugs as you are. You must be Uncle Skeeter." She made his name sound like a disease. "So nice to meet you."

Little Will and Tammy waited their turn in the introduction process. Ruth didn't appear to be impressed with them either. Bare-cheeked Tray she'd already met. But Uncle Skeeter seemed to fascinate her. At least she kept watching him as he scooped up the last of the catfish with a steel mesh strainer.

He had on black socks, his church shoes, shorts and a bowling league shirt with his fifty-year Sunday school pin proudly fastened to his collar. The church had had to have it specially commissioned. He hadn't missed a single lesson in two-hundred-sixty Sundays, and he'd buried three Sunday school teachers.

But I didn't explain the pin because I didn't think any of that would matter to Ruth McClaren. All she saw was an odd old man who probably shouldn't be left alone around grills and fish kettles.

When Skeeter scratched Leroy's ear and then repositioned a piece of fish on the platter with the same hand, Ruth made a small choking sound. Skeeter heard it and misinterpreted it.

"Don't be put off by Leroy. That missing leg is really my fault. The biggest raccoon I ever saw chewed it off." He shook his head and scratched Leroy's ear again. "I shouldn't have taken that bitch in season out hunting with us. Leroy was awful distracted that night. That's why the coon got 'em."

"Supper!" Mama yelled from the back porch.

Skeeter grabbed the pork chop and fish plates and headed for the house without breaking his conversational flow. "That's okay. I killed the sumbitch with a neat twenty-two shot through the spine. Had a hat made out of him. Finally gave it to Tray so he'd quit pestering me."

Ruth put her hand on Ian's forearm and gave him a look. I wasn't sure whether she was revolted at the image of a raccoon tearing apart Leroy's leg or the fact that Uncle Skeeter had a gun. What she didn't understand was that Uncle Skeeter had guns—plural. Every make, every model, for every hunting season. Each winter we lived in fear we'd find him dead in the deer stand.

But that was probably more information than Ruth needed or wanted, and I was fast losing any enthusiasm for sharing any family details with Ruth. Tammy sidled up beside me and whispered, "Bless her heart, she seems delicate."

To the casual outsider, Tammy might seem vapid and sweet, but she's as vicious as they come and a master of the "Bless her heart" insult. In the South, insults can be delivered without accountability as long as you preface them with "Bless her heart...."

The jury was in on Ruth McClaren. The family didn't like her, her attitude or her high-fashion suit.

Tammy's subtle insult had pretty much covered all the bases.

I should have defended Ruth. Really. I should have pointed out that she'd adjust. That she needed a little time. I didn't. I smiled and followed everyone in to a supper that couldn't be over fast enough to suit me.

Finally Ian seemed to get a clue and dropped back to be with me as we entered the dining room. He gave my shoulders a quick squeeze for support. Too little, too late, I realized. He'd been behaving almost as stand-offish and superior as his mother. Perhaps my expectations had been unrealistic, but I'd had this image in my mind of Tray on his shoulders and of Ian and Little Will smiling at some secret "guy" joke.

When we filed into the dining room, Mama cocked her head and started for the door. She opened it as the preacher had his hand raised to knock. "Brother Hollis. What a surprise! We were just sitting down to eat. You've come just in time."

"For supper? I had no idea your family sat down so early."

Claree snorted, not a bit worried about the preacher hearing her. "Every blessed day and you ought to know that because you eat here often enough. Now get in here before the food gets cold. And don't you try to sit in Elmer's chair again."

Brother Hollis' voice boomed as loudly in our home as it did from the pulpit. "Ah, Sister Claree, you are looking mighty rested."

She sniffed, but in the way of a woman who doesn't want to admit she's been mollified.

"Who's Elmer?" Ian whispered under cover of

the scuffling of chairs and rattling of silver as we settled around the table.

"My father." I pointed to the empty chair at the head of the table. "Mama keeps his place set at the table."

Ian stared at me for a second. "Is she nuts?"
Strike two.

"What a joyous day, Sister Shelby! Hope you won't mind if I give the blessing?" Brother Hollis didn't wait for an answer before he plunged into giving grace. I couldn't help but notice that the McClarens didn't bow their heads.

"Our Father, we thank you for the chance to work and grow the bounty of our table. We thank you for the strength to tend our fields and the strength to harvest our crops. We thank you for allowing us to cook this food to nourish our bodies. We most especially thank you for Sister Claree's wonderful way with the tea. Your bounty is a truly wondrous thing. Amen. Pass the potatoes!"

Mama hovered around the table, the tea pitcher in her hand. She wouldn't sit down until everyone had their drink and a plate full of food. I believe she judges the success of a meal by the level of chaos created by people as they wrangle and negotiate the expedited passing of their favorite dishes.

"Mrs. McClaren, let me pour you some tea."

"No." Ruth put her perfectly manicured fingers across the top of her glass. "I can't abide the syrupy stuff you people serve down here. But thank you anyway. Ian, be a dear and get us a couple of glasses of water."

Every Southerner at the table froze—some of them holding serving spoons suspended halfway between bowl and plate. No? Can't abide the syrupy stuff? You people?

I swivelled to look at Ian, certain he'd disagree and ask for sweet tea even if he hated sweet tea. He was, after all, the man I was going to marry.

Instead he hopped up from the table.

"Sure."

In the end, a simple beverage became the litmus test of our relationship. Sweet tea—the dividing line between us and them. I should have known it all along.

"Wait, boy." Aunt Claree laid her napkin by her plate and reached for their glasses. "The water might be pumped into the house, but it's still well water. You won't like it either unless we dress it up. So why don't I get the water? You run out front and grab a couple of sprigs of mint."

Claree's eyes met mine. The McClarens might have insulted the South in general, but they'd insulted Aunt Claree's tea in particular. Hell hath no fury like Aunt Claree in a snit.

I said nothing.

And while I know that remaining silent wasn't the most Christian thing to do, I didn't seriously entertain the idea of stopping Ian. What did it matter if he served his mother water flavored with mint Leroy christened on a regular basis?

It wasn't like I was going to marry the man.

Not anymore.

DINNER ON THE GROUNDS

The authors of **SWEET TEA AND JESUS SHOES** hope you will enjoy the following tastes of down-home cooking from family kitchens across the South.

All Human history attests
That happiness for man—that hungry sinner!—
Since Eve ate apples, much depends on dinner.

—Lord Byron,
Don Juan

Contents

Sweet Tea
Debra Dixon
—*Sweet Tea*

Fill metal tea ball (acorn shaped holder full of holes with chain on top) with loose tea. *Do not pack.* (You will learn what strength you like.)

In a small pan, put on 2 and 1/2 cups of water and bring to a boil.

Drop tea ball into boiling water, turn off heat, cover with saucer or plate and allow to steep for 15-20 minutes.

Drain tea ball over pan, then pour up hot tea into a large pitcher and add sugar to your taste (see below). Stir until dissolved.

Add 5 and 1/2 cups cold water and allow tea to cool completely before serving.

Fill glass with ice (ice always goes in glass first), pour and serve with a slice of lemon or a sprig of fresh mint.

Sugar: 1 and 1/2 cups for "treacly" really southern tea
           1 cup for medium sweet

Tip: Place a metal spoon in the glass before pouring the hot tea over the ice. This will keep the glass from cracking.

Sunday Ambrosia
Donna Ball
—Up Jumps the Devil

Ingredients:

1 3-oz. box lime gelatin
1 3-oz. box lemon gelatin
1 8-oz package cream cheese, softened
1 and 1/2 cups mayonnaise
2 cups miniature marshmallows
2 small cans crushed pineapple
1 cup chopped pecans
1 cup cherries, chopped

Mix lime and lemon gelatin together and dissolve in 1 cup boiling water. When gelatin is dissolved, add 2 cups cold water and place in refrigerator until semi-firm. *Do not allow to jell completely.*
In a large bowl, cream cheese and mayonnaise with an electric mixer until no lumps remain. Blend in semi-firm gelatin mixture. Fold in marshmallows, pineapple, pecans and cherries. Return mixture to refrigerator and allow to set for at least 3 hours. Great for family reunions!

Note: If you mix in the cherries before the gelatin is set, the mixture will turn brown. You can remedy this by adding a few drops of green food coloring.

Grandpapa's Cheese Straws
Deborah Smith
—Grandpapa's Garden

Ingredients:

1 and 1/2 cups sifted all purpose flour
1 lb. sharp grated cheddar cheese
1 stick margarine
3/4 tablespoon salt
3/4 teaspoon red pepper
1 teaspoon baking powder

Let margarine get very soft. Grate cheese and let it soften, also. Sift dry ingredients together. Start mixing margarine, cheese, and dry ingredients together until well mixed. Put half mixture in cookie press, making sure that no air is in the press by punching mixture with a knife. Squeeze out rows of the dough on a counter and cut into two-inch-long pieces. Bake at 350 degrees on ungreased cookie sheet until lightly browned on bottom. Let cool on wax paper.

If stored in an airtight cookie tin, the cheese straws will keep for weeks and the pepper will get hotter!

Vacation Bible School Sandwiches
Sandra Chastain
—The Jesus Shoes

Ingredients:

1 can potted meat
1 boiled egg, chopped
1 tablespoon chopped pickles
1 and 1/2 tablespoons mayonnaise
salt to taste
sliced white loaf bread

Mix first four ingredients. Spread to desired thickness on one slice of bread and fold in half.

Cow Patties   (Hamburgers)
Virginia Ellis
—Keeper of the Stick

Ingredients:

1 and 1/2 lbs of lean ground beef
1 medium onion
1/4 cup of favorite barbeque sauce
Splash of hot sauce
Garlic salt and pepper to taste

Break up hamburger meat into a bowl. Chop onion small—adjust amount to taste—and add to meat. Add barbeque sauce, hot sauce, garlic salt and pepper. Mush around with hands until thoroughly mixed. Make 5-7 patties and cook on hot grill. (Also may be cooked in a frying pan on the stove but it smokes up the house.) Remember, ground beef needs to be cooked at least medium done or the cows might bite you back.

Mama's Fried Chicken
Debra Dixon
—*Sweet Tea*

Ingredients:

One whole chicken, cut up for frying
1 cup flour
1 cup milk
2 eggs
1 teaspoon salt
1/2 teaspoon black pepper
1 teaspoon lemon/pepper seasoning
1 teaspoon garlic powder
1/2 teaspoon oregano
1/4 teaspoon sage
Vegetable Oil

Mix all dry ingredients until well blended. Add the eggs to milk and beat with a wire whisk. In a large skillet, add enough vegetable oil to be about 1 1/2 inches deep. Heat to 375 degrees. Maintaining the temperature is very important...remember that you may have to increase the heat if you add a lot of chicken at one time, then turn it back down when the temperature is right. Also, the larger pieces obviously have to be cooked longer.

Dip the chicken pieces in the milk/egg batter, then dredge in the flour mixture. Repeat, then put the pieces in the skillet. Arrange the pieces so that they don't stick together while cooking. Cook until golden brown on one side, then turn and finish cooking.

Steeplechase Potato Salad
Deborah Smith
—Flying on Fried Wings

Ingredients:

4 baking potatoes, cooked, chilled, and chopped into small cubes
2 boiled eggs, finely chopped
3 sticks celery, chopped
2 large dill pickles, minced
1/2 cup finely chopped bell pepper
3/4 cup finely chopped onion

Mix all ingredients with mayonnaise, mustard, salt, and pepper to taste.

Rat-tat-tooee, Southern Style
Virginia Ellis
—No More Mickey Mouse

Ingredients (No rats required):

1 good-size onion
2 medium zucchini squash
5 to 7 fresh okra pods
1 regular can of whole or diced tomatoes
1/2 teaspoon oregano flakes
Garlic salt to taste
Dash of favorite hot sauce

Pour enough water in a medium sauce pan to reach ½ inch in depth. Cut onion into one-inch chunks and drop into simmering water. Cut zucchini into 3/4-inch wheels, cut wheels in half again and add to water. Cut okra into one-inch wheels before adding to the pot. Pour in can of tomatoes, add seasonings and stir. Simmer for 30-40 minutes. (Eggplant may be used instead of okra.)

Mamaside Broccoli Casserole
Deborah Smith
—Nola's Ashes

Ingredients:

1 package chopped frozen broccoli (thawed)
1 and 1/3 cups of instant rice
1 can cream of mushroom soup
1/2 cup chopped onions
1/2 cup chopped celery
1 stick butter
1 8-ounce jar cheese spread
Bread Crumbs

Heat broccoli in 1/2 cup water and do not drain.
Cook and set aside rice.
Saute onions and celery in stick of butter.
Mix cheese spread and soup; Heat and stir until
well-mixed.

Combine all ingredients in a greased casserole baking
dish.
Dot top of mixture with butter and bread crumbs.
Bake at 350 degrees 45 minutes or until bubbly.

One-Eyed Cookies
Virginia Ellis
—Cookie the One-Eyed Horse

Ingredients:

2/3 cup shortening
2 teaspoons baking powder
1 cup sugar
1/3 cup whole milk
2 eggs
1/2 teaspoon salt
3 cups all-purpose flour
1/2 teaspoon vanilla
Assorted round decorations—M&M candies, unroasted hazel nuts or almonds, a dollop of jelly before baking, icing after, etc.

Mix shortening and sugar together until completely blended. Beat eggs and add to shortening mixture. Sift together the flour, baking powder and salt and add to mix alternating with milk. When thoroughly blended, roll out on floured board and cut circles with biscuit cutter or the lid of a medium-sized jar. Place chosen decoration in the center of each cookie forming an eye. Sprinkle with sugar and bake at 350-375 degrees for 10-13 minutes. Cookie would have loved these.

Missionary Society Strawberry Shortcake
Sandra Chastain
—Bigdaddy's Out House

Prepare a regular yellow layer cake recipe (Cake mix may be used, although the Missionary Society would frown upon it.)

Wash, remove leaves and stems from 1 quart strawberries. Cover the strawberries with sugar (about a cup, more or less) and set in the refrigerator until sugar melts and juice forms.

Whip one cup heavy whipping cream with 1/4 cup sugar and 1 teaspoon vanilla until stiff peaks form. Or you may use artificial whipped topping (but don't tell the ladies of the Missionary Society).

To assemble, cut layer cake into squares. Place each square on a saucer. Top with berries and juice. Place a dollop of whipped cream on each on. Garnish with a whole strawberry.

Mama's Pecan Pie
Nancy Knight
—A Little Squirrelly

Ingredients:

2 cups pecan halves and pieces (mostly halves)
1 and 1/2 cups dark corn syrup
1 cup sugar
5 tablespoons butter, melted
4 eggs
1/8 teaspoon of salt

Preheat oven to 350.

Combine eggs and sugar. Beat well. Add syrup, melted butter, and salt. Place one cup of pecan halves and pieces into uncooked pie crust. Pour syrup mixture over pecans and bake 45 minutes to one hour. Pecans should rise to top and brown.

Banana Pudding
Debra Dixon
—From Whence We Came

Ingredients:

8 medium ripe bananas, sliced
1 box vanilla wafers
4 cups whole milk
1 can sweetened condensed milk
4 medium eggs
1 cup sugar
1 and 1/2 tablespoons flour
1 and 1/2 teaspoons vanilla extract
Whipped cream

Blend eggs, sugar, and flour with an electric mixer on low. Increase speed to medium and beat until smooth. Add whole milk, sweetened condensed milk & vanilla extract, beat until just blended. Pour into a sauce pan and warm over medium heat, stirring constantly, until mixture thickens (5-7 minutes).

In a large glass bowl, layer vanilla wafers, banana slices, and custard. Repeat until all the custard and banana slices are used. Top with vanilla wafers. Serve chilled. Top with whipped cream.

Six Week Fruitcake
Donna Ball
—Fingerprints

Ingredients:

1 lb. flour
1 lb. sugar
1 lb. butter
12 eggs
1 cup molasses
3 tablespoons baking soda dissolved in 1 tablespoon water
1 cup grape juice or black coffee
2 tablespoons cinnamon
3 tablespoons allspice
1 tablespoon mace
1 tablespoon grated nutmeg
1 teaspoon cloves
1 tablespoon vanilla extract
6 lbs. raisins,chopped
2 lbs. dates, chopped
2 lbs. citron
1 lb. nuts (pecans, walnuts or almonds), chopped
1/2 lb. candied cherries
1/2 lb. candied lemon and orange peel, mixed
2 cups wine or brandy

(cont.)

Six Week Fruitcake
(cont.)

Dredge all the fruits in a mixture of flour and cinnamon. Mix butter, eggs, sugar and vanilla till fluffy. Add molasses and baking soda dissolved in water. Sift together flour and spices. Add alternately with grape juice/coffee. Fold in the flour-dredged fruits and nuts.

Fill two tube pans, leaving one inch at top for rising. Bake at 250 degrees for 5-6 hours. Test with toothpick until center is clean.

Cool for ten minutes by turning upside down on a soft drink bottle. Remove from pans. Pour one cup wine or brandy over each cake; wrap in a tea towel and put away for 4-6 weeks. Each week pour 1/2 cup wine over the tea towel to soak the cake.

Cakes baked between mid-November and Thanksgiving are ready to serve at Christmas.

Chocolate-Nut Pound Cake
Nancy Knight
—Uncle Clete's Bell

Ingredients:

3 cups of sugar
5 eggs
2 sticks of softened butter
3 cups of sifted flour (sifted 3 times)
1/2 teaspoon baking powder
1/2 cup of shortening
1 cup of milk
2 teaspoons of vanilla
1/2 teaspoon of salt
2 squares of chocolate, melted
1 cup of chopped pecans or walnuts
1/2 cup of pecan or walnut halves

Mix together flour, salt, and baking powder . Set aside. Pour milk and vanilla into a bowl and set aside. Cream sugar, butter, and shortening together well. Add eggs one at a time and beat. Turn mixer to low and add half of flour mixture and half of milk mixture. Beat completely. Add chocolate and continue to beat. Add remaining flour and milk, beat more. Finally, add chopped pecans.
Pour cake mixture into a greased and floured tube pan. Bake at 325 degrees for approximately 1 hour and 20 minutes until done.

(cont.)

Icing: Chocolate-Nut Pound Cake

2 cups of sugar
pinch of salt
1/2 cup of milk
1/4 cup cocoa
1 stick butter
1 teaspoon vanilla
3/4 cup pecan halves

Melt butter in milk. Combine mixture with sugar, cocoa, and salt. Bring mixture to a boil and boil for two minutes, whisking constantly. Remove from heat and add vanilla. Beat with electric mixer until thick enough to spread.

Note: Cake must be cool before icing. Ice cake. Arrange pecan halves on top of cake and serve.

To order additional copies of **Sweet Tea and Jesus Shoes**, contact BelleBooks:

Online: www.BelleBooks.com
                  Secured shopping.

E-mail: BelleBooks@BelleBooks.com
Phone/Fax: (770) 384-1348

Address: BelleBooks, Inc.
                  P.O. Box 67
                  Smyrna, Georgia 30082

Price: **$14.95** plus **$3.50** shipping/first class

Bookrate shipping free.
Georgia residents add applicable sales tax.

Seated: Nancy Knight, Deborah Smith, Sandra Chastain
Standing: Virginia Ellis, Donna Ball, Debra Dixon

We'd love to hear from you.

Visit our website at **www.BelleBooks.com**
for a little southern hospitality. There's always an
extra rocker on our front porch for a new friend.